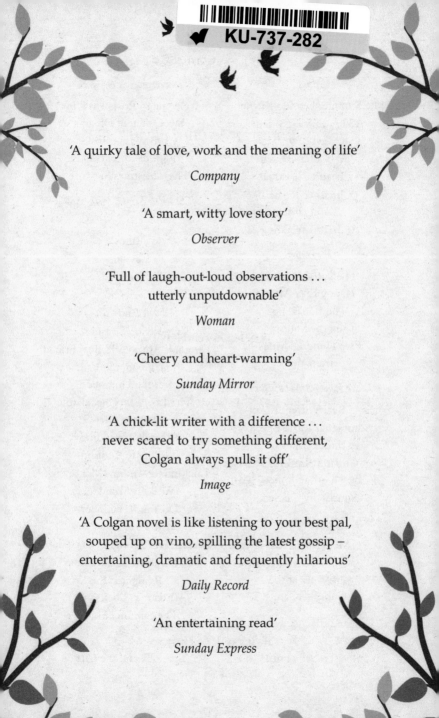

'A quirky tale of love, work and the meaning of life'

Company

'A smart, witty love story'

Observer

'Full of laugh-out-loud observations ...
utterly unputdownable'

Woman

'Cheery and heart-warming'

Sunday Mirror

'A chick-lit writer with a difference ...
never scared to try something different,
Colgan always pulls it off'

Image

'A Colgan novel is like listening to your best pal,
souped up on vino, spilling the latest gossip –
entertaining, dramatic and frequently hilarious'

Daily Record

'An entertaining read'

Sunday Express

Jenny Colgan is the author of numerous *Sunday Times* and *New York Times* bestselling novels and has won various awards for her writing, including the Melissa Nathan Award for Comedy Romance, the RNA Romantic Novel of the Year Award and the RNA Romantic Comedy Novel of the Year Award. Her books have sold more than nine million copies worldwide and in 2015 she was inducted into the Love Stories Hall of Fame. Jenny is married with three children and lives in Scotland.

For more about Jenny, visit her website and her Facebook page, or follow her on X and Instagram.

X @jennycolgan
 jennycolganbooks
 jennycolganbooks

JENNY COLGAN
Studies

Fourth Year at Downey House

SPHERE

SPHERE

First published in Great Britain in 2024 by Sphere

1 3 5 7 9 10 8 6 4 2

Typeset in Palatino by M Rules
Printed and bound in Great Britain by
Clays Ltd, Elcograf, S.p.A.

Papers used by Sphere are from well-managed forests
and other responsible sources.

MIX
Supporting
responsible forestry
FSC® C104740

Sphere
An imprint of
Little, Brown Book Group
Carmelite House
50 Victoria Embankment
London EC4Y 0DZ

An Hachette UK Company
www.hachette.co.uk

www.littlebrown.co.uk

To Laraine,
who makes everything possible

A Word from Jenny

I went to a very ordinary school that wasn't very nice at all. There was a lot of shouting and horrible remarks and fighting and belting going on (and that was just the teachers).

So that probably explains why I have always loved boarding school books so much. *Malory Towers*, *St Clare's*, *Frost in May*, the *Chalet School* books, *What Katy Did at School*, *Jane Eyre* . . . even *Harry Potter* when he came along. It seemed so exotic, so much fun.

Of course, when I met girls later in life who really had been to boarding school, they said it wasn't at all like that really, but I remain convinced that they were just trying to spare my feelings.

As an adult I found I still wanted to read these books – with, perhaps, some more adult themes, and maybe even – gasp! – some private lives for the teachers – but I couldn't find what I was looking for anywhere. So I have had to write them myself, and this is what you hold in your hand.

With love,

Jenny

x x x

Characters

Staff

Headteacher: Dr Veronica Deveral
Administrator: Miss Evelyn Prenderghast
Deputy Headteacher: Miss June Starling
Head of Finance: Mr Archie Liston
Matron: Miss Doreen Redmond

Cook: Mrs Joan Rhys
Caretaker: Mr Harold Carruthers

Physics: Mr John Bart
Music: Mrs Theodora Offili
French: Mademoiselle Claire Crozier
English: Miss Margaret Adair
Maths: Miss Ella Beresford
PE: Miss Janie James
Drama: Miss Fleur Parsley
History: Miss Catherine Kellen
Geography: Miss Deirdre Gifford

Pupils

Middle School Year Two

Sylvie Brown
Imogen Fairlie
Simone Pribetich
Andrea McCann
Felicity Prosser
Zazie Saurisse
Alice Trebizon-Woods
Zelda Towrnell
Astrid Ulverton

'You have been in every
line I have ever read'

Great Expectations,
CHARLES DICKENS

SUMMER HOLIDAYS

Chapter One

There is a reason why people don't like answering the phone. Because ever since it was invented, it can pass on the worst news known to man.

It can come at any time of the day or night – although little good is likely to happen if it rings at four o'clock in the morning.

It can come out of a clear blue sky or a dark rainy one. It can come when things are already troubling, or it can come when you are happier than you ever dreamt in your life you could be.

Maggie Adair, an English teacher at the famous Downey House school, sat in the car next to David McDonald, and as they crested the hill, heading off on their first ever holiday together, she felt full with terrified anticipation. She was brimming with happiness, but nervous too. What if he wanted to visit old ruins all day? What if he didn't appreciate how much she liked to lie down and read on holiday? What if he was funny about local food or talked loudly to the locals in an exaggerated accent?

He glanced at her.

'You look,' he said, 'like a woman terrified she's made a wrong decision by agreeing to go on holiday with someone she doesn't know very well.'

3

'I know you,' said Maggie timidly. And it was true. She knew he was a wonderful teacher. A kind and decent man. A reader. A . . . well, she couldn't think about the rest without blushing. Her bare white shoulders. A trembling mouth on the nape of her neck. She closed her eyes briefly.

That had seemed like a lot at the time. Certainly enough to throw up her whole life; ditch her fiancé, therefore upsetting her entire family back in Glasgow, both by throwing over someone they loved very much, and refusing to leave the Cornish boarding school she taught in to move back to Scotland to teach in what her sister Anne called a 'real school'.

She had given it all up to follow him, follow her heart. And here they were, and suddenly it felt – not an anticlimax, but rather, something terrifying. She had been in love with him for three years; or at least, in love with an idea of him – his broad smile, his dark, dancing eyes, his long lean frame . . . yes. All of that.

And on David's part, he had caused a scene at a railway station that had got him arrested and cost him his job; he had given up everything, including a fiancée, and now worked at Phillip Dean, a badly rated school in the area that had trouble holding on to any staff at all.

But now – Maggie could barely believe it – they were actually here, driving away in his car.

Was this . . . was this for keeps? Experimental? All her friends who were on dating apps talked a lot about how many men they met who seemed amazing, perfect on paper, but then vanished into thin air soon afterwards. After all, David had been engaged to somebody else . . . as had she, of course. Were they both all-in?

'Do you want me to tell you the really annoying stuff first?' said David. She looked at him, trying not to let the anxiety show on her face.

'Oh goodness,' he said. 'This is bad. Let's see. I wear a panama hat in the sun otherwise I freckle.'

'I don't mind that. Or freckles. I have lots.'

'Well, that's a first,' said David, frowning a little. 'Uhm, I will always take a train or a boat rather than a plane if I can.'

Maggie smiled. She didn't see him as someone who got up at 4 a.m. to catch easyJet flights. Although she herself was, very much so. She had always loved her girls' trips.

'What's wrong with that?'

'Well, it can take me a rather long time to get anywhere.'

Maggie looked out of the car. It had a creaky old canvas cover – it was ancient, Maggie hadn't even thought they made Saabs any more – and they had pulled it down, so the beautiful Cornish lanes were flitting past them, the wild roses dancing in the light summer breeze, the scent of their petals heavy on the air.

She had pulled the tie out of her long curly red hair – she always wore it up at school – and David enjoyed it streaming behind her, glorious in red and gold and amber. He wanted to bury his hands in it, had to force himself to concentrate on the road.

'I don't think you doing things slowly presents much of a problem,' said Maggie, looking at him and going rather pink. He glanced at her with a sudden jolt and blinked in the sunshine. It was a very quiet road. There were passing points and plenty of high bushes. He was sure they could pull over ...

Maggie looked at him, her breathing coming a little faster, then impulsively reached out and put a hand firmly on his long thigh. They both looked at it. And that was the exact second the phone rang.

Chapter Two

At first she couldn't hear over the roar of the air and the tears and crackling down the phone.

Then her heart plummeted as she heard it was her sister, Anne, who was trying to get words out over her sobs. As if in sympathy, the sky overhead had suddenly darkened across the moor, clouds moving in at speed from the sea.

'What is it?' said Maggie, desperately. 'What is it, Anne? Is it Cody? Dylan?'

A cold hand grasped at her heart, thinking of her beloved tearaway nephews.

'No, no,' said Anne. 'No – it's Stan.'

Stan: Maggie's ex-fiancé. A decent salt-of-the-earth man who had never done anything wrong (apart from drink the occasional beer too many and go on about Celtic a bit too much); who had suspected the truth long before Maggie could bear to admit it, even to herself; whose disdain for the long thin Englishman – and disbelief that Maggie could ever have chosen him, a viewpoint shared by most of her own family – had been particularly hard to take.

'What? What's the matter with him?' Maggie swallowed hard.

'He's been in an accident. At work.'

Stan worked in a paper warehouse, often night shifts. It

was tough, manual work, poorly paid, but he had always enjoyed the camaraderie of his work mates, and it was decent, honest labour, as he had always pointed out during their many fights about whether or not she was getting above herself.

'Christ! Is he OK? What happened?'

Anne debated with herself. She was, and had made no bones about showing it, annoyed with Maggie, had been ever since she'd moved three years ago. She'd gone off to this posh boarding school without glancing back at all the deprived schools in her own home town that could do with a dedicated teacher, which Maggie undoubtedly was.

Instead she was wasting her talents on spoilt, pampered princesses who already had every conceivable advantage in life – you could even stable your own pony at Downey House – rather than where they were desperately needed. Anne's own children had to make do with substitutes and locums – Cody had had three primary one teachers and could barely read at eight years old. Anne worked ten-hour days in her own hair salon as well as bringing up the boys single-handedly, and keeping an eye on their ageing parents. She thought Maggie's choices extraordinarily selfish, particularly when she'd thrown over Stan, whom they'd treated as a member of the family for ten years, for some fey Englishman who read books and seemed just as devoid of responsibility as Maggie herself.

Maggie never asked after Stan at all, was too full of this new man, whom she tried not to mention too often in Anne's presence. But Anne could tell she was happy; she looked wonderful, she was bubbling over, evaporating with happiness, and she couldn't stop it spilling out.

Meanwhile Anne was still cleaning up the mess Maggie had left behind. Maggie had dumped Stan with a wedding dress hanging on the back of her door – had jilted him at the altar, more or less – and then swanned back off to sunny Cornwall. She'd left Anne to comfort their confused mum, and explain the situation to the many cousins and uncles and aunts that made up the wider Adair family.

And if Stan was drinking too much, and was driving a forklift with a hangover, and wasn't sleeping much at night because he'd been left by someone he thought he was going to spend the rest of his life with, and someone had done some lazy careless stacking. Well then. It was hardly surprising there'd been an accident.

But all she said, because she was a good sort, Anne, was that he had crashed his forklift into a large set of pallets, that had crashed down on his head, and that the doctors had put him in an induced coma.

David stopped the car. A light summer rain had started to fall and he put the roof back on the car as Maggie walked up and down the road, talking to her sister, her face a mask of dismay.

He found a waterproof coat in the boot and put it round her shoulders. It was as if she didn't notice him.

'Do you think I should come?' she was asking Anne, who sniffed.

'Well, obviously not if you're *busy*,' she said, sarcastically.

'I don't . . . I didn't mean it like that,' flared Maggie, whose temper could lie close to the surface. 'I mean, do you think he'll want to see me? When he wakes up?'

'Reckon,' said Anne.

There was a pause.

'I'm on my way,' said Maggie. 'Oh God, Roy and Pam.' They were Stan's parents.

'They're in pieces,' said Anne.

'Oh Christ. They must be. They won't want to see me though,' said Maggie, worried.

'Don't be stupid,' said Anne. 'They want everyone who cares about Stan.'

'Of *course* I do,' said Maggie. 'Of course I do!'

Tears ran down her face with the soft rain, and David watched her, terribly terribly worried, leaning against the car, as he got soaked without even noticing.

They had been going to catch the ferry from Plymouth to Santander, meander in the convertible across southern Spain, France, down to Italy, enjoying every second of the long summer break, eating local cheese, and boar, and freshly picked tomatoes, and lemon-scented fish, and reading and drinking rosé in the sun; making love in any roadside inn or farmhouse they could find; turning brown and languid with love and wine and food and one another, all summer.

In comparison, Southampton airport on the first day of the English summer holidays, with screaming kids everywhere and long queues and an incredibly expensive flight for Maggie to Glasgow, and some kids from Phillip Dean somehow being there, and shouting filthy remarks every time he as much as tried to hold Maggie's hand – even though they only meant it in fun and he didn't really have the heart to tell them off for it.

It was the heartbreaking opposite of everything Maggie had hoped for, and her heart was breaking for Stan.

'Are you sure you don't want me to come?' asked David. 'We could drive there by tonight. Or I could leave the car here, nobody's going to steal it. It's older than all my pupils.'

Maggie shook her head.

'I think ... '

'I'd do more harm than good?'

'It's just . . . '

'I know, I know,' said David. 'I am so so sorry.'

'It's not your fault.'

'I know. I'm just . . . I'm sorry it's such a mess.'

'Maybe I'll get there and he'll be sitting up in bed asking for a sausage roll and what the Celtic score is,' said Maggie.

'I'm sure that's the case,' said David. 'I'm sure it is.'

They stood, awkwardly, at the long departure line, the noise and the dinging announcements and annoyed people and general low-level stress and anxiety of any airport, especially in the school holidays, making it impossible for David to say what he wanted to say, with Maggie so distracted, glued to her phone.

There was a silence neither of them knew how to fill.

'What will you do?' said Maggie.

'Wait for you,' said David. Then, as she passed into the queuing line, held up with long dirty strips of elastic that children kept tearing down, he kissed her, firmly but chastely.

And she thought he might say 'I love you', which Stan had told her, so often.

But he didn't.

Chapter Three

Felicity Prosser's mother didn't really get cross, per se. She considered it both bourgeois and the kind of thing that encouraged wrinkles, and Caroline Prosser was nothing if not a great combatant in the battle against wrinkles.

This, however, had left her rather askew. Which would be putting it mildly.

Their beautiful country house, in its two acres of immaculate lawn – the sliding back window leading on to the slate terrace; the wild flower meadow she'd had specially imported; the island kitchen and chill-out room – all of it was covered. In empty bottles, ash, stamped-out cigarettes, ends of joints, mud, dirt, badly cleaned-up red wine vomit, red wine, not-even-cleaned up red wine vomit, broken plates, bits of pizza the dog hadn't got to.

And Fliss Prosser curled up fast asleep, with some other languid forms dotted around the utterly wrecked sitting room.

'FELICITY PROSSER!'

If there'd been any more glass to break in the house, Caroline Prosser might have broken it.

'A *party*? How very nineties of you!'

Fliss's long-suffering father had been summoned home

from London, where he was working. Caroline was meant to have been at a spa, but had come home early as her favourite aesthetician had selfishly gone off to have a baby, and the replacement wasn't up to scratch.

Only to discover ...

Fliss was managing to both cower and look defiant on the sofa at the same time.

Hattie, her hated and perfect older sister, came downstairs.

'I told her not to! I had nothing to do with it.'

'Who'd want to party with you?' sneered Fliss.

'Shut up, both of you,' said their mother. Fliss had never seen her so cross. 'I mean, what the HELL were you thinking?'

'It was only meant to be a few people.'

In fact, Fliss had had big plans. She was going to look awesome, everyone from school would be there, and they'd all think she was amazing and super cool for having a party and she'd meet someone lovely and get off with them in front of everyone and it would be brilliant.

Things had not happened quite like that.

'Did you put it on Facebook?'

Fliss snorted, even though – from the number of people who had turned up, mostly thirteen-year-olds from the village who thought there might be free cider – clearly somebody had.

'Christ no. Nobody's on Facebook.'

'Well, I bloody wish you had put it on Facebook then. How is Rosita going to clean all this up?'

'I didn't think you were coming back till tomorrow.'

Fliss was suffering through her first ever hangover and not managing very well. She wanted to be sick.

'Why should Rosita clean it up? Why should she?' demanded Hattie.

'Shut UP,' said Fliss.

'No. *You* be quiet. Right now,' said Caroline. 'Your father is going to be furious.'

Fliss had never known her father be furious about anything, so she sat still with her arms folded, her mouth a mutinous line, trying to remember everything that had happened the previous evening.

Simone had thrown up in the garden, she remembered that much. Oh God, so embarrassing. Ismé was meant to be coming and hadn't shown up. Alice and Will had arrived hand in hand in his new sports car, like they were proper stupid grown-ups or something, looking incredibly glamorous, noticed all the thirteen-year-olds and had, like, one glass of their own Champagne then whizzed off again somewhere much fancier, as if her friends were just too dreadfully dreadfully childish for words, and it had made her feel worse than if nobody had come at all.

There were absolutely lots of local kids – word had got around – whom Fliss hadn't seen since Brownies, which was embarrassing. They were over-impressed with the house and behaved like total rubes, as did Simone, who could never quite get over the interior-designed vastness and newness of her home, with the plumpness of the cushions, the perfection of the placing of the vases and how spotless it all was.

Well, had been. It wasn't looking like that now. There'd been high jinks in the swimming pool too, which would now have to be drained, and some very suspicious-looking upheaval in the flower beds.

'You're grounded,' said Caroline, her face white with anger.

'I'm grounded anyway,' hurled back Fliss. 'You sent me to boarding school, remember?'

'Well, *quite*,' said Caroline, her voice icy. 'Look what you do to my home when you're here.'

'Your home!' shouted Fliss. 'Yes, YOUR home. We all know it's YOUR home. Not ours!'

And she stormed off, slamming the door, leaving her mother, plumped-up mouth gaping like a fish, staring around at the devastation, as well as several groaning teenagers waking up and emerging from various guest bedrooms, all of which would now have to be fumigated.

It was going to be a very long day for Rosita.

Chapter Four

The flight from Southampton was short but felt endless, the little propeller plane droning low over the green summer landscape, turning cloudier as they got further north. Maggie had thought maybe someone might be there to meet her at the airport, but nobody was. Busy, of course.

It was a lot chillier in Glasgow than in Cornwall, even in July, and drizzle was falling as she shivered, stepping off the little steps of the plane into the shiny terminal, filled with happy-looking families and round cheerful children heading off on their normal holidays, to Malaga and Tenerife and Florida.

Maggie moved against the tide, it felt like, realising that her bag was full of clothes that would be useless now; floaty dresses and light white shirts and big sun hats and saucy underwear – she had rather splurged – that would have been perfect for meandering their way across Europe, drinking Aperol Spritz and taking long siestas in cool shadowed rooms with religious statues and lace mats.

Well. No point in thinking that now. She layered on two T-shirts and a shirt in the airport toilets and strode towards the bus station, jutting her chin out against the wind, wondering about what she had left behind – already it felt like a chimera, a dream she had once had, something about which there was nothing remotely solid – and heading into the harsh reality ahead.

The hospital was shiny, new, astringent-smelling, wide corridors full of lumbering people, heads low; charging doctors, loud cheery nurses. Maggie tried to follow the signage to the High Dependency Unit, and found it at the very end of an extremely long corridor.

In contrast to the bustle of the corridors and lifts – the crying babies, the chattering relatives – everything in HDU was quiet and calm, apart from the bleeping of machines and the slow breathy noises of ventilators.

The staff here were not jolly or urgent, but instead careful, measured, practised. In a strange way, Maggie thought, their charges were more like the machines they were plugged into: bodies, yes, but something to be kept running smoothly, to be adjusted and changed and moved and regulated like a finely tuned engine. It was both odd and reassuring at the same time.

It was easy to see where Stan was; his was the bed that was completely surrounded. A nurse sniffed.

'Only two people at the bedside,' she said, rather crossly. Nobody took the slightest bit of notice, as his parents, Anne and her own parents all stood up.

Maggie had never felt so far out of the family; both families, in fact.

If they'd got married last summer, when they were meant to, none of this would have happened, probably, because everything would have been different. Stan might have had another job. There might have been a babby at home, even. He wouldn't have been working those night shifts then. Everything would have been different. The air felt thick with blame, and Maggie felt herself shrivel inside.

*

There were quiet, careful, consolatory hugs. Maggie felt tears sting her eyes as she saw Aggie, Stan's sweet mother, who'd never been anything other than kind to her, since school days.

'I'm so sorry,' she said, smelling the familiar Yardley scent.

'Wasn't your fault,' mumbled the woman, as convincingly as she could manage. Maggie hadn't seen her in a year or so, but she'd aged terribly.

'Glad you could make it,' sniffed Anne.

'You called me eight hours ago,' Maggie couldn't resist returning. Obviously if she'd been living in Glasgow, where she belonged, she'd have made it a lot faster, was the implication.

She decided to ignore all that and sat near Stan. His parents left for a while to get themselves a coffee – or get themselves out of the way, Maggie knew; to avoid a difficult atmosphere.

'Should I talk to him?' she said, as she looked at him on the bed. His head was half shaved, his ginger hair stark against the deathly paleness of his skin, and the bottom of his face was slack. He didn't need a shave, which was odd, as he normally did; his mum must have done it.

Anne shrugged.

'Can't hurt,' she said. 'Well. Depends what you say.'

She gave her a warning look and Maggie felt insulted. As if she was going to sit here and brag about her new life ...

The idea that she might, finally, after all the torment of the last three years, actually have something that might constitute 'A New Life', that might actually be something you could dream of looking forward to, that there was a future in sight, that she could see how it would work, how her life would unfurl ...

Oh, Maggie. Never make plans.

In the sterile, beeping hospital ward, Maggie picked up Stan's hand, and stroked it, and said, 'Hello.'

Chapter Five

The English summer was hot and drowsy. In Surrey, Fliss was on no-speaks with everyone after the party, as well as being grounded, which made things pretty lonely, to the point where she did the absolutely unthinkable, and requested if she could go up to London to stay at Simone's.

Caroline rather wanted her out of there and couldn't imagine Simone would be particularly rowdy, so let her go with a wave of her hand. There were of course plenty of more suitable friends of the Prossers with whom she could stay, Caroline pointed out to her long-suffering husband, but Fliss was determined to have a proper urban experience, and could not be dissuaded – and she was nearly sixteen.

The trip was not a success. Simone panicked about it and her house for days on end They had a little terrace in Tottenham, with two bedrooms upstairs, and a tiny box room that belonged to her brother Joel, who played computer games in there and basically never came out and it smelled absolutely dreadful all the time.

Downstairs there was a kitchen and a living room, where the smell of her mother's cooking permeated – Fliss's house, she thought ruefully, only smelled of expensive scented candles – and there were boots and shoes lined up in the hallway and their cat's litter tray and oh, gosh, where would Fliss even sleep?

Simone had a trundle under her old single bed that she'd had since she was tiny, for visiting relatives. Fliss had a double bed in her own room plus there was a guest suite Simone had stayed in that was utterly palatial, with its own bathroom and a gushing, claw-footed bath with as much hot water as you wanted and when you ran a tap it didn't immediately mean someone else screaming because their shower had gone cold.

Her mother, she could tell, was equally anxious, because she started buying things they never normally had in, like branded toilet paper and potpourri, causing Joel to stomp around the place making remarks about stuck-up snobs.

All in all it was a slightly anxious place to welcome a guest, particularly one who was already rather highly strung. When Fliss found out that Ismé – the new girl from the year before on whom she had the most terrific pash – was out of town, or rather, was saying she was out of town, and being very quiet on her Instagram, she was rather starting to regret everything before she'd even started, particularly when she asked Alice where to go in London and Alice had immediately started namechecking the Bluebird Café and all sorts of places that were simply miles away from Simone's house.

Poor Simone had to listen to a LOT about Alice and Ismé. Ismé she liked, Alice she was utterly terrified of, but either way she was completely incapable of getting involved in the kind of wallowing bitching session Fliss was clearly in the mood for. Neither did she have much in the way to offer in slagging off Fliss's big sister Hattie and she couldn't hide her horror of the way Fliss talked about her mother. The idea of talking about anyone's parents in that way was too awful to contemplate. Fliss did a lot of heavy sighing. She'd messaged Alice. *Maybe we can go to Camden and get tattoos*, she'd suggested, at which Alice had messaged back, *Oh, bless* in a way which made Fliss wish they weren't committed to sharing a room with Alice again next year and wondering if all teen girl friendships were like this.

It wasn't, really, Fliss's fault that she was shocked by Simone's house. She had been brought up by parents who had also been brought up to expect everything; who had had everything they'd ever wanted. She hadn't, Simone supposed, asked to be spoiled – and Fliss, Simone knew, felt practically deprived next to Alice, whose divorced parents every so often married other people and were almost never around, and who had been more or less dragged up by nannies and a limitless credit card.

But Simone felt she could have worked rather harder to disguise her shock that Simone's family only had one bathroom. Or that she was expected to sleep on a trundle on the floor (the way Fliss tried to laugh it off, mentioning how 'charming' she thought it was, was not, in fact, any more helpful; she sounded like the Queen doing her best to make do).

Despite begging her not to, Mrs Pribetich had prepared a massive table of food. Fliss had said, 'Can't we just get a pizza or something', but suggesting ordering pizza in the Pribetich household was basically a massive insult to every single member of it. Simone had mentioned Fliss's eating disorder but Mrs Pribetich was of the generation that didn't quite believe in them, or at any rate thought that if they did exist, it was just because they hadn't tasted her cooking yet – there was a vast array of dishes of Armenian food; dumplings swimming in oil; bulgur wheat salad, warm scented flatbreads.

Of course Fliss looked at it with the same stupid duchess-opening-a-fête face on and picked two or three tiny morsels.

21

Of course Joel sniggered and stared at her lasciviously and made remarks. Of course – of COURSE – her mother bigged up Simone's predicted straight As at GCSEs and asked Fliss how she herself had done, as if that was ever the kind of thing you talked about – 'MU-UM,' Simone had said, and her mother had said, 'Well, I'm just telling the truth, sweetie' and then gone on to mention that Simone had a boyfriend, did Fliss? And when Fliss had said, stoutly, that she was 'bisexual and not really into like a gender binary?' had totally failed to hide the confusion on her face rather than being impressed like Fliss had hoped.

It was forty-five minutes on the tube into the centre of town and Simone completely failed to notice how unused Fliss was to public transport. Fliss had never come up to town on her own before and her mother just conjured black cabs out of thin air, as far as she knew – and the mad tramp shouting in the carriage and the crush of people up and down the lifts felt like some kind of pointed comment on her life, Simone reflected, retreating.

Simone withdrawing into herself of course made Fliss feel more awkward and self-conscious than ever and it wasn't helped when they finally hit Topshop at Oxford Circus, which was absolutely heaving, and Fliss wanted to try on lots of things and Simone couldn't get anything over her size G bosoms, which still showed absolutely no signs of slowing down and it seemed like there was nothing, absolutely nothing, she could do about it.

Standing in the boiling changing rooms, nodding as Fliss tore on and off tiny scraps of material crossly, barely waiting for whatever Simone might have thought, complaining vociferously about how 'fat' she looked, Simone's heart sank as she felt their friendship drifting away.

Things perked up slightly when Fliss insisted on treating

them to the rotating chocolate sushi bar then deteriorated again when she complained constantly about how naughty she was being and barely touched a thing.

Simone was exhausted and she'd neither bought anything nor opened her mouth apart from to insert fewer chocolate cakes than she would genuinely have liked in order not to look like a pig.

Fliss then insisted on taking a black cab to Camden Town, in which Simone sat, frozen with fear every time the cab stopped in traffic, hypnotised by the counter whizzing round and terrified Fliss would ask her to pay half, which, given that Fliss had absolutely no idea about the value of money, was quite possible, but Fliss had her parent-funded debit card and was feeling no compunction about abusing it, so Simone had sweated her new make-up off for nothing.

Camden Town was scary, full of white people with dirty dreadlocks and dogs on pieces of string, and gothy teenagers with crazy make-up and boot shops that smelled weird and sold weird stuff and neither of them knew quite what to make of that either, and Fliss sighed and they both tried to pretend that this was quite cool and they were having a good time but, deep down, neither of them were.

It made matters slightly worse when, home again, Fliss having once more refused to eat more than a little bit of side salad for supper, they were flipping through Instagram – Fliss had made Simone open an account; Simone mostly posted the neighbourhood cats – when Fliss couldn't help letting out a little moan of despair.

'What?' said Simone, leaning back from her small desk chair – Fliss was on her bed.

Fliss simply showed her the phone. It was Alice at a party, tagged Chelsea, with a lot of incredibly glamorous, much older people, at a clearly over-eighteens night spot.

They sat in silence for a while. Fliss was burning up in humiliation and rage. I mean, Simone, sure. She wouldn't expect to get an invite. But her and Alice ... they were meant to be friends!

Chapter Six

Simone, meanwhile, was in despair. She alone of all of them had a boyfriend – a serious boyfriend, someone she was in love with. He was called Ash, and he was small, fierce, intense and incredibly clever.

The worst, however, had happened. After a short break-up last year, Ash had faked a suicide attempt to get them back together. To the absolute surprise of both teenagers, all the adults they knew had gone absolutely bananas about his doing this – they'd been studying *Romeo and Juliet* and as far as they were concerned, it was simply common sense.

None of their teachers or parents had seen it quite like this, however, and Ash's father – who was raising him alone – had retaliated, despite their tears and imprecations, by taking him out of school and sending him to a day school near his home, where he could keep an eye on him, now Ash was old enough to let himself in and make his own tea.

They were both devastated. Hundreds of miles apart, without even a glimpse in school chapel or at mixed events; no more Friday-night mixers or field trips, only social media, which was both useless and, in Ash's case, banned until he could stop having hysterics. Ash was helping neither of them by continuing to have hysterics.

Simone was utterly bereft. She didn't mind being a

shoulder to cry on for Fliss or the other girls; she had always known she had Ash and they were solid and she didn't feel so alone for having the largest breasts in the school, or having to pluck her monobrow almost constantly – which she was sure made it come back even coarser and worse – or being poor, even though people made such a big deal over pretending she wasn't poor or that it didn't matter to them which made it, like, a zillion times worse.

But her and Ash being separated was terrible, and it was worse that Fliss was there because they couldn't email each other ten times a day and talk about how awful it was.

The second Fliss finally departed, the entire Pribetich household let out a massive sigh of relief, even though they kept it secret. And Simone went back to working in the restaurant, where, the very next night, Ash came charging in.

'What!'

'Ssh! My dad is at the garage round the corner.'

He pulled her into the alleyway behind the restaurant. He was yet to get his growth spurt. Ash explained he absolutely didn't mind as his huge brain was going to take over the universe anyway, *and* he liked being not much higher than Simone's bosom very very much indeed.

'You should stop working,' he growled in his funny man's voice. 'I'm making like a ton of money from crypto. I can just give you some of that.'

'Dad needs me,' said Simone, pushing back her hair.

'How was Fliss?'

'Gruesome.'

Ash sniffed with satisfaction.

'Well, I'm here now.'

And they embraced in the dirty old alleyway.

'It's only till we turn sixteen,' he whispered, checking his watch.

'Did your dad say that?' said Simone.

'Oh. No. But I can legally divorce him then. And we can get married in Scotland. Hypothetically.'

'I'm glad you added hypothetically,' said Simone.

'Ssh,' said Ash. 'I still can't believe they're making us take GCSEs.'

'It'll be interesting.'

'No it won't,' said Ash. 'We'll both ace everything and I'll be another year off designing a new supercollider.'

Simone wondered, not for the first time, how Elon Musk's girlfriends managed, kissed him passionately, and sent him off back to his dad's car.

Chapter Seven

In Scotland, the days melted into one another; wet, dreary. Maggie would go to the hospital. She would have liked to have seen some of her old friends, but really because she and Stan had been together since school, all of their friends more or less had been joint and it was very awkward. It wasn't that anyone blamed her, but she'd been away for three years. She'd chosen to move country, to be with other people, while they saw the same people they'd always seen, lived near their parents and their siblings, had Sunday lunch round their mum's every week, had bought lovely little starter apartments, still affordable in their area, and were popping out babies whose names she didn't remember.

She envied them in a way. In many ways.

David was writing to her – more or less every day or so – all handwritten notes in his beautiful handwriting, or just a few words on a postcard. He had gone to Europe for want of something to do; tried to share the experience with her in every way.

Her mother was always up earlier than her, bringing her elaborate airmail lettergrams and sniffing, as if sending handwritten letters was somehow showy or over the top. And although in any other set of circumstances she'd have been thrilled, bowled over even, she was furious with herself for not being able to be more simply delighted by them; to just enjoy the experience – someone she adored was sending her love letters, often with funny little sketches in the margin of a dog he'd seen, or the woman in the panettone shop, or a new panama hat he wanted to buy, what did she think?

They made her laugh, but also embarrassed as her family seemed to view each one as some effete intrusion that was totally inappropriate in light of everything that was going on, and Maggie could see their point of view as well.

But she couldn't tell David to stop writing: he was her life, her link to a happier world than this, where things were so serious with Stan. Over that damp, dank summer, in shades of mild grey, though, things gradually started to improve. A twitch of an eye here. A small curl of the fingers – which seemed to have started retracting into themselves like claws – and the doctors were saying they were going to attempt to bring him out of it. The swelling on his brain had gone down and it was time to wake him up; see if he'd be OK, if Stan was still in there. The more Anne and Maggie read about brain injury, the more frightened they got. There was a settlement from the company he worked for – apparently some of the boxes had been wrongly stacked – but would it be enough, if he came back impaired, couldn't look after himself, had to move into his mum and dad's, be in a wheelchair, need washing, dressing, feeding? It was beyond frightening, and the doctors could tell them very little to lift their spirits.

The day they attempted to wake Stan, Maggie babysat her nephews. Anne was going; Maggie wouldn't be appropriate, she knew. She tried instead to lure Cody and Dylan away from their devices – where they spent every second they could – worried about how little they read. She offered to read them a story and they stared at her as if she'd suggested they go down a coal mine and work all day. Both the boys

29

were pasty-looking, as if they ate too much brown food and stayed indoors too much, and Dylan, the older, already had a pot belly that was larger than it ought to be, even on a little boy. Maggie couldn't begin to imagine how much Anne would kill her if she ever mentioned it. Their parents spoiled their only grandchildren, as well they might, while Anne was working all the hours God sent to keep everything together.

Another way in which she'd failed, Maggie reflected, as they were glued to an extremely noisy Xbox game that was apparently a certificate 18 – she'd run away and left them all. She suggested going out to play football, but the rain was tipping down and the idea was quashed pretty fast.

She glanced at her phone. She should call David. But, one, she didn't know where he was – he'd been doing some Don Quixote pilgrimage thing and his phone, never particularly reliable at the best of times, had been very much in and out; and secondly, this was meant to be the very beginning of their relationship. The fun, loving, sexy, getting-to-know-you bit. Not the 'Oh, my ex is in a coma and everyone thinks it's your fault' bit. She didn't want to be a downer. Plus she needed to keep the line free for the hospital.

She sighed, and kept staring at the phone.

And finally it rang. And shortly, her face was wreathed with smiles.

'It was the oddest thing,' Anne couldn't stop babbling as Maggie charged into the hospital, a boy in each hand. 'He just moved his head! And he said, like he was asleep, he said . . . '

Her voice trailed off.

'What?' said Maggie, then realised Anne's face was twisted.

'He said, "Maggie".'

Maggie bit her lip. She'd been afraid of that. She was slightly hoping that he'd wake up and be fine except for some mild amnesia which meant he'd forgotten her completely and anything that had ever gone on between them.

But Anne seemed so pleased.

'And then ... and then he blinked and said, "No ... Anne." He recognised me!'

Maggie was genuinely delighted. 'Oh my God, that's wonderful!'

'He fell asleep again. But I phoned you anyway. They reckon he's coming out of it! He recognised me! He can't *totally* be a vegetable!'

'No,' said Maggie, 'no, he can't. Thank God.'

And indeed, it felt like a waterfall gushing through her insides: of insane relief, coupled with the horrible, tiny voice deep inside her that thought it might be her fault, and that other people thought that too.

On the ward, everything was a fluster. Stan's parents standing with an arm around each other and their other hands on Stan's. His eyes were open and he had a sleepy, slightly confused look Maggie recognised only too well from many, many weekend mornings.

Even though life changed, and things moved on, nothing could erase their time together, she knew, as she went round to the other side of the bed and, disregarding the stares and looks from other people, kissed him gently on his hair, which smelled of girls' shampoo – how very kind the nurses were.

No matter what happened, he had been part of her life. For a long time. And there would always be love there, even if it changed its shape. Great loves of your life, even if he wore a Celtic strip most of the time and had fallen under his own forklift truck ... they were a part of you.

'Hey,' she said. 'I'm so glad you're back.' He blinked, looking at her. 'Maggie,' she said.

'Aye, I ken that,' he said, then gave her a half-smile. 'I didn't think you'd be here.'

Maggie bit her lip.

'Well then,' she said.

'But Anne . . . '

'Yes, yes, everyone else has been here, I know,' said Maggie, feeling guilty. 'I'm glad they were.'

'There are too many people in here,' said a nurse, bustling them out, and Maggie watched regretfully as Stan was enfolded into the arms of his family.

And finally, she felt a little less guilty about the fact that in less than a week, she was due back at school.

Chapter Eight

Scotland had had a wet summer, but Cornwall had had an absolute beauty: good waves for the surfers; good sunshine for the bathers. Every little cottage had been booked; every hotel doing smashing business as going abroad seemed more and more of a hassle, and staying in the UK more and more tempting.

Downey House, nestled in the little valley over the crest of the hill, overlooking the sea at the bottom of the steep cliffs, was gleaming and ready for business once more.

Dr Deveral had let it be used for several weeks as management retreats for an MBA course, not because she particularly approved of that kind of thing in the building – alcohol, people staying up late, etc – but because they paid a frankly vulgar amount of money to do so, all of which she could pour into maintaining the house and the grounds without having to bump up the fees. Some of her girls were rich, obviously. But some were from families that were making sacrifices – grandparents chipping in – to get something they felt their children needed, whether it was music tuition, vanished from so many state schools, smaller class sizes or sporting facilities.

Dr Deveral had no illusions as to whether it was fair. In fact, what she was pretty sure was not fair was the dearth of opportunity and rigour in state schools. But they wouldn't have a place for an old dinosaur like her.

Regardless, even Miss Prenderghast, her faithful PA, noticed she had a spring in her step as she walked through the doors, examining every single thing with her customary sharp eyes, checking for dust, or unblinking smoke alarms, the click of her heels – Dr Deveral never wore flats – the only sound in the empty corridors.

Everything seemed in fine order, however, and they were doing well in enrolment numbers too, despite the downturn.

She smiled to see Dr Fitzroy, her opposite number as head of Downey Boys, a mile over the hill, waiting for her in her office. He was frowning from under his shaggy hair. Spotting other people's emotional states was not exactly top of his skill set, but he sensed something different in his colleague.

'Veronica,' he said. 'Did you have a good summer?'

'Excellent, thank you,' said Veronica briefly, not wanting to get into it. 'Brushed ... brushed up on my Russian.'

Once again, she was smiling to herself. Miss Prenderghast was very confused. Her boss smiled both rarely and, generally, only ironically.

'Good, good. So, ready for the new term?'

'I think so ... how's our reprobate?'

She was referring to Mr McDonald, the young English teacher who had caused such trouble with her own English teacher the year before.

'Still a bolshevik,' growled Dr Fitzroy crossly. 'He's not coming back.'

'You're joking,' said Veronica. 'Maggie's coming back here.'

'I know. Nope. He says he's needed at the comp, and they've got some plan to force-integrate some of our sessions. Mix all the children up.'

'I saw that,' said Veronica. 'It's best we do, don't you think?

We're going to have to do outreach of one kind or another; it makes sense to do it with one of our own in situ.'

'Will be nothing but trouble,' predicted Dr Fitzroy.

'Good,' said Dr Deveral, and once more Miss Prenderghast gave her a curious look.

Chapter Nine

The train was awkward, to say the least. The worst of it was, Fliss had gone back to Guildford (sending Simone's mother an elaborate thank you card, which surprised that good woman mightily, as she had been fretting non-stop about the terrible time the poor young underfed girl had had) utterly crestfallen.

Once home, she was still not talking to her mother, who, irritatingly, wasn't giving in for once and was spending her time taking Hattie on expensive shopping expeditions or to tea, all of which Hattie lapped up. Hattie usually felt totally ignored as the well-behaved daughter: everyone generally tore around after Fliss as she got herself into one scrape after another. Added to this, Hattie always felt the sting of her mother – extremely slim and elegant and petite – bequeathing her butterfly figure and yellow hair to her younger daughter, rather than Hattie's down-to-earth somewhat more yokelish genes of her farmer's-son-done-good father.

But to Fliss, worst of all, Alice, her partner in crime, Alice, her supposed *Best Friend*, hadn't been in touch with her, even after Fliss had sarcastically commented on her Instagram post, then deleted it, then unfollowed Alice then followed her again, then put a love heart next to the post. Fliss had been reasonably sure that doing one of these things would have triggered something, but Alice seemed relentlessly not to care.

Fliss was furious with her. Alice not having noticed was the most aggravating thing of all.

So by the final day of the holidays, following an incredibly expensive two weeks in a Tuscan villa where almost none of the four of them – Caroline having tired rather quickly of Hattie's hockey chat, and missing her bitchy, funny, grumpier daughter – were really very interested in talking to one another or hanging out at all, and their father spent most of his time on the phone to his office, Fliss was both desperate to see and desperate to avoid Alice.

As fourth-formers they were allowed to take the Paddington train, which was heaving with schoolgirls, hockey sticks, violins, stray scarves and a lot of loud shouting as she approached.

Fliss felt an icy feeling in the pit of her stomach that reminded her very much of her first day at Downey House, when she had also been absolutely furious with her parents for daring to send her there in the first place. Although she had eventually learned to like it. Well, so she had thought.

She saw Alice walking, as usual, as if she was on a catwalk in Paris rather than dressed as a schoolgirl coming through Paddington station at eight o'clock on a dull September morning. And to her absolute and clear irritation, she was walking with Ismé, the beautiful girl who'd arrived last year, been stationed in their dorm and who had gone on about how privileged and spoiled they all were.

Fliss had instantly developed a massive crush on her which Ismé had treated with the kind of generalised disdain with which she treated everything else. She was the main reason Fliss had got her hair cut which, Fliss was sure, was why she looked too young to get in everywhere and why

Alice had so thoroughly dumped her all summer. Ismé, on the other hand, had long tumbling ringlets and coffee-coloured skin and was, all in all, probably the most beautiful girl Fliss had seen in her entire life. She sighed. This was going to be tricky. Alice, oblivious, raised an exhausted hand.

'Good God,' she said as she approached. 'Another year in the gulag.'

Ismé rolled her eyes. 'How spoiled would you have to be to think Downey House is a gulag?'

'All right,' said Alice, whom it was impossible to insult. 'We're not even back yet, no need to start your tellings-off before we've even had to endure the train.' She put both hands up. 'Please don't tell me what percentage of the world's population have never even been on a train. Hi, guys!'

'Hi, Alice!' said Simone, blushing loudly, as she wasn't quite sure what was the loyal thing to do to Fliss and what was least likely to attract Alice's sharp tongue. She was terrified of Alice.

Alice glanced at the two girls and realised immediately that there was something up with Fliss, and sighed internally. Always with the drama. Whatever it was now, she hoped Simone would sort it out and smooth it over, as she usually did. She had a lot of respect for the quiet, stalwart girl, not least in the amount of homework copying she got to do, even though she'd never noticeably shown her affection. Dragged up by a succession of nannies while her mother followed the summer around the Med, showing affection was something all of the Trebizon-Woods girls had trouble with, which, coupled with their English rose Helena Bonham-Carter-style beauty and haughty attitude, was making them irresistible to an entire generation of young Englishmen.

'Hi, Fliss!' she said in her cheeriest voice just to be

annoying, which she was. 'Right, shall we cram on board? God, I can't believe they won't let us go first class any more.'

It was true. After a rash of girls upgrading themselves to first class on their parents' credit cards, and the more daring attempting to order gin and tonics from the harassed train staff, it was now banned completely and there were two assigned carriages near the middle of the train where they could sigh, grumble, bitch and apply make-up to their hearts' content without annoying anyone.

'Please tell me your mum packed you some good tuck,' she said to Simone, who blushed as usual and held up the massively overstuffed hamper her mother had sent her with in case of a siege – and the others cheered.

Chapter Ten

In the end, they were so near the end of the holidays that Maggie and David decided to meet up just before they went back.

Everything she had planned to say all summer had gone unsaid; every moment she had dreamed of spending in his arms ... The fact that they had got together at all now felt like a bizarre idea, from far away, not something real. The idea of being relaxed and easy with him felt utterly impossible – as if they were starting from further back than she'd ever been. She had spent her entire summer babysitting under a grey and miserable sky, or hanging out in a hospital, buying her mum fruit scones and drinking endless cups of sweet tea. She did not look her best, she knew. She felt so provincial, not at all like the exotic people David must have met on his travels – sometimes, in her worst moments at night, her imagination conjured up a luscious Spanish woman, with long thick black hair and enchanting black eyes, a Penelope Cruz. Or a slender, chic French girl, like her friend Claire, drinking pink wine with her bare feet dangling in turquoise waters.

After all, who, as far as she was concerned, wouldn't want David? Maybe she was an idiot to have let him roam free all summer, she thought at her saddest. But on the other hand, that was ridiculous to think; she couldn't be like that. And if a few weeks was all it took for him to get over her, well, was there anything there to begin with?

It didn't stop some very, very difficult nights and quite a lot of general insomnia, none of which helped her look her best either.

They arranged to meet up again at Reuben's, the noisy, cheerful surfer bar that employed young people from difficult backgrounds in Looe, a couple of days before the start of term. Maggie had never been more nervous about anything in her life. It was a first date they'd never had.

On David's part, he had been a little puzzled by her more than muted response to his missives, but was on the whole used to being the slightly awkward person in the relationship and didn't feel he should pretend to be the kind of person he wasn't, i.e., somebody who used Snapchat and liked viral videos and was on social media all the time. He knew these things existed, and tolerated them (except in his own classroom) but didn't use them.

He was, though, terrified of how things had gone with Stan, who he knew was thankfully on the mend. He had spent the summer annoyed to be seeing beautiful things that he would have loved more than anything else to experience with Maggie for the first time. Annoyed in yet another beautiful tiny cathedral at the top of an ancient hill in Spain, on a whim he had enrolled himself into a stable and learned to ride a horse, something he had never taken to as a shy, bookish child; his father, a senior officer in the army, and his brother, now a commander in the navy, had both been boisterous, rugby-playing types who had adored hacking across the country but he had always been the odd one out, even more so when his mother, his stalwart defender, a gentle,

41

bookish woman he adored, had died of breast cancer when he was thirteen.

He had thrown himself into books after that, earning his degree and his PhD very early, turning down the cloistered worlds of academia that were on offer to him in a quest which even to the most amateur of psychologists was clearly to stop any other thirteen-year-olds ever from feeling the same way he had. He couldn't believe he'd finally met someone who seemed to like him exactly as he was. He didn't know if he could bear it if her feelings had changed.

Maggie, late and frazzled from the traffic, was absolutely terrified. It was worse than a blind date. What if … What if … What if after everything they'd been through, he'd changed his mind?

She put on her prettiest dress; a light green. Here in Cornwall in September it was as warm as it had been in Glasgow in the middle of July.

She caught sight of him wandering along the shoreline, the warm late-summer sunshine illuminating everything in dripping lines of gold, and cursed gently to herself.

He was brown as a nut; hard-bodied from learning to ride. She smiled to herself remembering how he'd told her about his pony, Cioccolato, which had hated him and tried to bite him every time he went anywhere near it, and thrown him off several times, and now he was doubting the wisdom of everything he'd ever read about human–horse relationships but he didn't feel that being apologetic was helping him status-wise with Cioccolato.

Nonetheless, a couple of cuts and bruises seemed to suit him. Maggie couldn't help it. Her face broke into a huge beam. She jumped up and down and waved like a lunatic and, when he saw her, couldn't restrain herself. Despite being a grown-up school teacher, at an ancient school that prided itself on turning out decorous young ladies, she dropped her cardigan and ran full length across the promenade, into his waiting arms.

AUTUMN TERM

Chapter Eleven

Miss Starling, head of English, was extremely annoyed, even by her standards. First Dr Deveral had barely appeared to be listening when she, June Starling, had gone through her excellent reasons for why she thought Miss Adair's suggestion of relooking at the syllabus to steer it away from being too white and Anglo-centric was weak and ill-judged, as was everything else that common Glaswegian girl did. Dr Deveral had looked miles away, sighed and said, yes … perhaps *Anna Karenina*?, at which June had said, for GCSE? and Dr Deveral had said, no, well, she supposed not, but it truly was the most devastating novel, didn't she feel? and June had sniffed because as far as June was concerned, literature was made to be parsed, explained, put in the correct boxes of the correct things to say about it to earn a starred A, and anyone could do that if they only paid attention to the nuts and bolts, so whether you found something devastating was useless at best, distracting from the task at hand at worst.

And now here was Miss Adair again, turning up like a bad penny, despite her scandalous behaviour. Breaking up an engagement for a teacher at the boys' school! It had been awful. Particularly as that young man had lost his job over it. If anyone should have lost her job it should have been

Maggie, with her incomprehensible accent and an upbringing that made her chippy.

Not to mention the fact that everybody knew Maggie's house class, now fourth years, were by far the worst-behaved. But did anyone listen to June? No. Even worse, Maggie was positively glowing; grinning like a Cheshire cat at every returning child, asking if everyone had had good summers; embracing that annoying French teacher Mademoiselle Crozier as if they were great friends (they were: Miss Starling didn't really understand work friendships) .

Maggie stood up on the old stage at the opening night assembly, looking round, remembering, wonderingly, how nervous she'd been in the past; how intimidated. But three years at Downey House had changed her, she knew. This was her home; her school. She was a part of that. The terrified first years who had sat cross-legged in the front were now her beautiful fourth years, and it was them she was talking to.

'This is a big year for you fourth years,' she started. She looked at them. Simone, as usual, looked almost as terrified as she had done in first year. Despite easily coming top of every class she was in, being a surprisingly useful hockey goalie and a nice writer, even if her spelling could be a little erratic, Maggie wished she'd believe more in herself. Perhaps if she could get an exceptional set of results, that would show everyone – including that old witch Miss Starling, who had looked at Maggie sourly, and muttered something under her breath about her having spent the summer living in sin that Maggie hadn't quite managed to catch in full. If only she knew, thought Maggie, but she wasn't going to drag more of her dirty linen into work if that was OK with everyone.

'You have your exams at the end of this year – I know you've already done half the work, but this is where it really happens. Before you know it, it will be your mocks in January, and time goes fast. Make every moment count, and I know I can trust on your commitment and maturity to see you through.'

Alice rolled her eyes at this but realised, to her annoyance, that Fliss wasn't returning the eye-roll. Oh God. The last thing Alice wanted to do was to get into a big girlie pow-wow about the whole summer and why she hadn't asked her friend, who looked about twelve and was prone to tears every five minutes, to social events with her big sisters. She found the tearful travails of teenage girls a little . . . wearying, which was annoying, as she was plainly trapped inside the body of one for the foreseeable.

'Remember I'm here for you, as is the entire team,' said Maggie, not noticing the very clear wince Miss Starling gave at the very concept of a 'team'. 'Don't let yourself get overwhelmed. We'll see you through this, OK? That's what we're here for.'

This was Maggie's first year group of her own she was nursing through exams, and she was genuinely nervous about it. There was an informal competition that ran through the staff – not encouraged by Dr Deveral, but not discouraged either – to see how many of their girls would emerge with A stars.

Maggie didn't want to push fragile girls beyond their limits, or add to various pressures on their lives that could really upset their equilibrium, as if being sixteen wasn't its own problem anyway.

On the other hand, she didn't want to see any of them perform below their potential; otherwise, why were they here?

Maggie was catching up with Claire, who shared her sitting room in the teachers' apartments at the top of the building, and was a dear friend of hers. Claire had rather a lot to say about the current political and economic European situation, and Maggie was pretending to listen, having enough problems of her own right now, but they both found this a typical and rather relaxing state to be in, so neither minded.

They put up new postcards, and Claire burst out laughing as she caught sight of a picture David had sent Maggie that had been taken at the riding yard and showed him riding bareback in only a thin white shirt on a large brown horse. Claire's laughter was raucous and, blushing furiously, Maggie immediately hid it back in her things.

'You are so so funny, *ma copine*, but ah ... ah cannot look at that, *non*? Eet ees not ...' She laughed again. 'You know, he ees teacher. Not Vladimir Putin.'

'Stop it!' said Maggie good-humouredly. 'I just thought it was a good photo, that's all.'

Claire rolled her eyes.

'Eet ees good, my friend. Eet ees good you see him this way. Let me ... let me see it again.'

'*No way!*' said Maggie, zipping her bag firmly. '*Pas de chance.*'

'As he comes galloping to scoop you up ... in zis style so *masculin* ...'

Maggie was still pink and giggling as she heard a knock on the door. It was very unusual for one of the girls to disturb them after hours, but not unheard of and certainly not forbidden.

Fliss was standing looking woeful in the corridor, her eyes huger than ever in her face with her little gamine haircut not grown out yet, just messy – Maggie thought it looked cool; Miss Starling had wanted to mention it at the assembly in terms of things that were banned. Maggie couldn't help but feel her heart sink a little. Fliss was sweet enough but seemed to attract trouble wherever she went. There was a fragility about her, a lack of being able to deal with the day-to-day travails of growing up in a way her stolid sister Hattie, or her eminently sensible friend Simone, seemed better able to bear.

'Hello there, Felicity,' said Maggie. She guided her to a window seat at the top of the stairwell, not feeling quite ready to invite the child inside while her belongings were strewn everywhere and she hadn't unpacked her own under-pants. 'What's up?'

'I wondered . . .' said Fliss, nervously. She wished her voice didn't wobble so much. 'I wondered if I could change dorms.'

Maggie frowned.

'But dorms were allocated yonks ago – I thought everyone was happy.'

Fliss bit her lip.

'I just fancy a change.'

'Is this about Ismé?'

Maggie knew all about Fliss's crush. Fliss coloured.

'No,' she insisted.

'Have you fallen out with Simone?' Fliss shook her head. 'Alice?'

The silence was deafening.

'OK,' said Maggie. 'Felicity, I understand this is unpleas-ant. It must be horrible. Girls do fall out. You know it's a normal part of adolescence – probably the worst part, in my opinion. It's horrid. But the best way to get through it is to work it out – have a screaming fight or a discussion or just something. Don't leave it to fester, then it will just last so much longer.' She looked at the girl's face. 'Do you feel she's been bullying you?'

Fliss shook her head.

'Has she used language towards you that you found upsetting in any way?'

Fliss shook her head again.

'Well, in that case – you've been great friends for a long time. Just think of all the fun you've had!'

At this Fliss's lip wobbled and Maggie realised she'd got it completely wrong.

'And now she's just dropped me!' said Fliss. 'Because I don't look eighteen!'

'You don't,' agreed Maggie. 'And quite the best thing too.'

But Fliss was sobbing now and Maggie desperately wanted to give her a cuddle, but of course did not.

'She's dumped me.'

Maggie's heart was full of sympathy. Being dumped by a friend could be every bit as painful as being dumped by a boyfriend; more so, because nobody took it as seriously. But the issues the girls faced, however trivial they seemed to the outside world, were very real to them.

'That is harsh,' said Maggie. 'So tough. Are you sure it wasn't just the summer? And now you can go back to normal?'

'But then she'll dump me again!' wailed Fliss.

Maggie thought of pert little Alice and considered this to be an entirely true statement. She sighed.

'Won't it just cause more upset if you move out?' she said.

'I don't care!' said Fliss. 'I don't want to see her.'

Maggie's face was rueful.

'OK,' she said. 'Listen, there's nothing spare just now, I'm afraid, the school is completely full. Why don't you quietly ask around and see if anyone will swap with you – don't pressure anyone, just ask nicely, OK? And then we'll see. And I'm afraid you're just going to have to bear it until then.'

Fliss nodded, looking martyred, but Maggie felt she was a little cheered by having her concerns taken seriously.

'Female friendships are difficult,' Maggie said. 'It's part

of being a woman. They are good, passionate, strong, loving things at their best, and really tricky at their worst. Do your best. And remember, you have many strengths Alice will never have. Try not to compare yourself too much.'

Fliss nodded blankly.

'Well, I suppose I could just hide in the library and do extra prep,' she said, standing up.

'Well, there you go,' said Maggie, taking her literally and smiling a little. 'Silver lining.'

And she went back inside feeling rather pleased with herself, and completely unaware that she had just made a terrible mistake.

Chapter Twelve

Fliss was absolutely boiling with frustration. When would people stop telling her just to grow out of things? Or that it was a phase, or that there was nothing to be done?

She stumped back to the dorm, where Isha and Alice were having a ridiculous fight about politics which they were both plainly enjoying very much. Simone of course was up to her ears in books. She sighed. Down in the common room Astrid Ulverton was playing her clarinet and people were yelling at her to shut up while they watched a Korean boy band perform. Oh God, they were so *basic*, thought Fliss.

Furious, she opened her phone in the corner and found herself helplessly scrolling through Alice's Instagram. Alice on yachts. Alice and Will in trendy beach bars at sunset. Alice laughing with a group of her sisters and their friends including ... yeah, he was tagged. A young hot actor who was currently in a huge Netflix historical drama. Alice hadn't even mentioned it to Fliss, even though she knew Fliss loved that show. Fliss stared at it for a long moment. Then she deleted the app off her phone, made up a fake email address on a Gmail account, and relaunched herself as the first name she thought of, which happened to be Seo-Joon, one of the young Korean singers. All the better, thought Fliss, putting her region as Seoul. Who would suspect her?

Her fingers were trembling. She followed a few random accounts that showed up, some Kardashians, then found her way to Alice's account. Underneath all the fawning messages from friends and fellow students – and plenty of people Fliss had never heard of; Alice had a bit of a following among people who liked girls far too young for Instagram on yachts – she typed in, 'omg, basic like?' and, before she could stop herself, pressed 'reply'.

She sat back, horrified by herself, glancing around, sure everyone there would know what she had done. To traduce someone on Instagram was breaking every code there was; to do it under a false name. Well.

But she felt better. It purged something. It changed the mood she was in. Feeling shaky and somewhat bold, she finally felt ready for bed.

Chapter Thirteen

The first morning was the usual scramble of lost shoes and lacrosse nets; rushed breakfasts and complaints about the breakfast (even though on the first day back they got bacon and sausages as a special treat before the menu reverted to porridge, cereal, fruit and toast); lost files and people fighting for their turn at the hairdryer and the mirror, putting on the tiniest amount of allowable make-up and lots of shimmer and bronzer designed to show off summer tans, not to any boys, of course, but to the other girls in their class. Everyone was in a rush, adrenalised and slightly late, not least the teachers. It was time to re-enter the fray ...

Maggie scanned the class. Who had grown, who had already had the odd nose job under the guise of some sort of sinus difficulty, who looked ready to face the year and its challenges. She had caught Alice going in that morning and, trying to sound casual, had asked if everything was all right with Fliss.

Alice, in that usual way she had of confidently talking adult to adult – she'd had it since she was eleven, Maggie had always found it disconcerting – had simply rolled her eyes and said, 'That girl needs to get off with someone more desperately than anyone I have ever met,' and continued down the corridor, Maggie staring after her.

Now Maggie smiled at her class.

'We're going to be looking at Dickens this year,' she said. *'Great Expectations*. And then *The Scarlet Letter*. It's about the terrible corrosive nature of gossip and sniping, so I imagine it will have absolutely nothing to do with contemporary life.'

A few wry smiles went round the room.

'And,' she added, as blithely as she was able, aware that the girls had an incredibly heightened ability to sniff out any sign of gossip, 'remember that for this year, for certain subjects, notably drama and sport, you'll be sharing for the first time with our partnership school, Phillip Dean Academy in Darne.'

There was a gasp at this, even though it had gone out in the newsletter.

'But!' said Simone, mortified suddenly. 'But it's *swimming* this term.'

Maggie blinked. She hadn't really thought that one through. Phillip Dean, of course, was co-ed.

'Well, we won't be doing co-ed swimming,' she said hurriedly, even though in fact she wasn't a hundred per cent sure about this at all. The parents would go up in absolute uproar.

Mind you, there was absolutely nothing wrong with co-education. But she took one look at Simone's utterly miserable face, with her totally-unasked-for huge boobs, and imagined her faced with a group of what by any accounts were fairly rough boys – it was a failing school that David was desperately trying to turn around – and could immediately see both points of view.

The swimming row blew up more emphatically than anyone could have seen coming. David was incandescent.

'Basically what you're saying is that all my boys are sex pests,' he said, folding his arms.

'I'm not saying that!' said Maggie desperately. 'Downey Boys and Downey Girls don't even mix for swimming!'

'Well, maybe they should,' said David. 'Everyone has to learn how to be civilised.'

'At the expense of my girls?'

They were trying to have a quiet supper in the pub in the village, which was tricky enough as any of the school staff could see them at any point, making them both jumpy.

Also Maggie was on breakfast duty, which meant she couldn't come back to Exeter and stay over in David's flat, which was in any case minimalist to the point of troublesome. Her apartment in the school was cosy and homely, but of course him entering the premises was completely out of the question, and they couldn't both afford to keep going to hotels all the time.

'So you think women need to be segregated from men?'

'No!' said Maggie. 'But David, it's an all-girls' school. They chose that, and therefore they don't expect to have to swim with boys, that's literally the point. I mean, anything, *anything* other than swimming costumes, seriously.'

David looked mutinous and picked at his fish. He had a fondness for very plain food that Maggie normally found endearing but was currently finding slightly annoying.

'I mean, can you absolutely absolutely promise they'll behave themselves?'

David toyed a little more with his fork.

'I can ... I can absolutely do my best,' he said.

Maggie winced. 'I'm not sure this is going to fly. One off remark and we might be looking at a court case.'

'So the very first thing that Phillip Dean and Downey House are meant to be doing together is doomed to failure. I suppose my girls won't be allowed to swim with the Downey boys' group either?'

'There's lots of other sports,' said Maggie.

'Yes, but we promised them swimming – most of them don't have any access to that at all. Most of them can't swim, Mags.'

'Oh God, that's awful,' said Maggie, shocked. She thought about it. 'We could certainly find spare sessions.'

'So then they get ignored by the snobby children on the very programme that's meant to make them mix!'

'Did I or did I not just say there's *loads* of other sports?'

David counted them off on his fingers.

'Archery, hockey, rugby, lacrosse, pony riding ...'

'Cross-country running?'

'That we already do,' said David. 'It doesn't cost anything.'

They lapsed into silence.

'I'll speak to Janie James,' said Maggie, thinking of the jolly PE teacher. 'I'm sure she'll come up with a solution. You speak to Nicholas.'

Nicholas Craig was head of boys' PE.

'He's training Olympians, as usual,' said David. 'He won't want to give up a second.' He sighed. 'OK then, what about the Christmas show?'

'Oh,' said Maggie. 'They've got mocks right after the break. We weren't going to do one.'

David folded his arms.

'So, nothing then.'

'Can we talk about something else?' said Maggie, wearied.

David wanted to curse himself. He had sworn blind they wouldn't just talk about teaching all the time; it was dull and impossible and all he wanted to do was get to know her – herself – instead of constantly worrying about their charges.

He leaned forwards and tucked a rogue curl of Maggie's bright red hair behind her ear.

'OK, sweets,' he said. 'I'm sorry. We'll figure something out.'

'I know,' said Maggie. 'Sorry. Argh! It's just work, isn't it?'

'It is,' said David. 'Tell me about you. How are things at home?'

He meant Downey House. The school had always been a home to him.

Maggie thought he meant Glasgow and was surprised but pleased he'd asked.

'Oh, much better,' she beamed. 'Stan's up and about, making incredible progress, doing his physio. The doctors are delighted with him, reckon he'll be back at work after Christmas. They're sticking him in the back office, where he'll keep out of trouble, Anne says. She's there most days still, I think. He's just got so many people around him, it's a miracle really.'

'OK, good,' said David, drinking a glass of water. 'Uhm. I'm pleased to hear it.'

There was a slight pause, and then David took out a book and for a horrifying moment Maggie thought he was going to start reading at the table but in fact he wanted her advice about something and suddenly, once more, they were back on an even keel again, laughing and joking and sparring about what he was reading and what each other hadn't read, and it was normal again. But not, one would say, exactly resolved.

Chapter Fourteen

David had stridden back into Phillip Dean Comprehensive on the first day of term, astonished at how changed he felt about everything. When he'd started there last year, in disgrace, he'd been worried and upset how things would go. Yet coming back now, having chosen to not return to Downey Boys, knowing people here, feeling the difference in the air, even as the autumn chill had begun to bite, he felt optimistic, despite the downtrodden, chaotic air of the vast crumbling comprehensive, its single-glazed windows rattling in the breeze, its staircases picked and pitted with holes in the cement, with old graffiti and gum under every desk and handrail. Even with all this, he couldn't dampen his natural exuberance.

He could feel it in the air. And following his disappointing summer – well, disappointing in some ways, as Maggie had not been with him, but in others, like learning to ride, for example, oddly satisfying – she was coming back! She was coming back! He had been extremely worried that she would change her mind; decide her heart and her life was in Glasgow. And to be honest, could he really have blamed her?

Darker and more upsetting, he had wondered what would happen if Stan had – God forbid – died. He couldn't let himself think of that at all, couldn't let selfishness cloud his judgement. His overwhelming relief when Stan had woken up, was going to pull through, had not been, he knew, entirely altruistic and full of concern for his fellow man. It freed Maggie to come back to him. Even if it didn't feel like home to her, which worried him still.

But even so. And Phillip Dean, unlovely even in bright autumn sunlight, the colour on the trees turning orange and red – that didn't feel like anyone's home. But it was, he knew. To some children whose home lives were worse than you could imagine; with no security; whose parents had to visit food banks to keep them fed; who would turn up in the depths of winter without socks or proper coats.

David had never realised what a sheltered existence he led. When he'd started teaching, he'd taught in state schools – but generally nice ones, in nice parts of town. This was the very first job he'd taken as a teacher who hadn't been able to pick and choose, as a teacher who didn't have ideals. David did have ideals: to communicate the beauty and universality of literature to young minds; to open them up enough to take it in.

He had never dreamed of being a caretaker to children; to being *in loco parentis* to them. He loved literature primarily, and cared about imparting this love, to enrich lives in the way he desperately believed poetry did enrich lives.

But the Phillip Dean kids – not all of them, but some of them – didn't need literature. They needed the very basics of life: food and shelter. To try and fill them with Shakespeare felt like, at most, a secondary gesture. He was having to turn into a different type of teacher. Possibly even a different type of man.

A large round of applause went up when Barry Frise, the downtrodden headteacher, made his usual mumbled address at the beginning of the academic year, in front of a rather motley collection of pulled-together uniforms. The girls all seemed to be wearing black trousers so tight they outlined every single bit of their bodies, which surely couldn't have been in the original uniform brief. There were no ties, huge ties, tiny ties and shirts in varying degrees of whiteness. It was as different to the freshly scrubbed identical rows of Downey Boys as could be imagined, and the air smelled of Lynx, hairspray and feet.

Yet David was pleased to see them all, and touched that they were pleased to see him. Teachers came and went at quite the rate at Phillip Dean, and everyone had known he was only there because he'd been suspended. The fact that he'd come back of his own accord meant something.

'Hello, everyone,' he said, looking out particularly at his home room class, 4R. 'It's a big year! Exams, lots of work, lots of fun.'

There was some embarrassed shuffling and a few groans. Phillip Dean was at the bottom of the league tables for exams, absolutely miles below, even when free school meals were taken into account. It felt almost embarrassing to mention it, and many teachers never did.

'I am so excited at how much better we're going to do than the predictions,' David went on remorselessly. 'We're going to show them all.'

He smiled at Pat, the music teacher, who had seen her hours cut and cut and now skulked about like a dog expecting to be whipped; they were allies.

'Also, Mrs Carr here and I have a new plan that is going to do a lot, I think, for us. You know before this I was at Downey House.'

There was a mass booing.

'SNOBS!' shouted one loud newly broken voice from the back.

63

'That's enough,' said David mildly. 'Regardless, they have very kindly agreed that from this term on we're going to be teaming up and forming a joint programme with them.'

The school went silent, interested.

'They have plenty of facilities that I feel we ought to share. I think we have a lot to learn from them . . .'

There was a fair amount of low-level grumbling about this.

'And I think they have a lot to learn from us too.'

At this there was general laughter.

'Yeah, about twocking cars!' came one voice.

'OK,' said David, with a slight edge to his voice. 'I'll be letting you know further details in the fullness of time, but for now, I think anyone who's interested should start by signing up for choir.'

Choir had been the compromise after swimming was resolutely not going to fly, and with the lack of a Christmas show. It was, everyone agreed, a start. And they could do something nice at the end of term. The hope was that the Downey parents would be happy at the outreach, especially the guiltier, *Guardian*-reading tendency, and that the PD parents would be pleased to see more organised events than the zero that currently happened. There were a lot of fingers crossed. But could they possibly get the children on board?

Chapter Fifteen

The weeks slipped by with terrifying speed as the school shook itself down and put itself to work, settling into a brown and chilly autumn, damp with slippery leaves and wet rain, leaving the lazy dreams of summer far behind. The air smelled of mud and pencil sharpenings.

David had not wanted to walk past the choir sign-up sheet. If there really wasn't any interest in the two schools mixing, it was going to take an astonishing amount of energy to make up for it.

Also, he would absolutely hate it if he got the usual small group of clever, committed children, marginalised by the other kids. What if he only got them – lovely little Clément, with his glasses fixed with sellotape, who was in third year and still didn't look like he was ready for secondary school at all; big, pink-faced Mattie, constantly blushing at everything she did, even though she wrote with insight and elegance (and couldn't take a compliment without blushing; even more than David had found himself having to get used to making people blush, working in a co-ed for the first time).

Fond of them although he undoubtedly was, what if he had to take a little band of misfits, and the big, confident rugby-playing Downey House mob took the piss out of them relentlessly and made everything worse, his children getting rejected twice over? That would be awful.

What he really needed was one of the cool kids to help him out, someone who would get everyone else behind them. He sighed and went to have a word with the unofficial head of the football team – Phillip Dean wasn't organised enough to have an actual official football team, tragically. The local council had sold off the grounds, and there wasn't any requirement to take sport after second year, as a result of which many of the increasingly rotund children simply dropped it: the girls certainly did. Having to get into a hockey skirt after puberty was simply not worth the catcalls. It was, David reflected, a great shame. Sport helped teenagers more than they could ever understand at the time.

There was no need to spot who the coolest kid in Phillip Dean was.

Calvin Hopekirk was coming off a playtime kicking an old ball when David summoned him and asked for a word. Six foot two at fifteen, he was a good-looking mixed-race boy who lived with his grandmother for reasons David was unaware of, but he imagined they weren't good.

None of this ever showed on Calvin's face. Some children took this kind of thing out in violence or bullying others. Calvin took it out on the football field, where he was absolutely lethal. In class he was gentle as a lamb: he turned in no homework and took almost no interest in school business, but without malice; he was diffident, but charming, slightly disconnected, but not a bad lad, not a bully. The bullies avoided him because of his size and popularity, in fact. The girls liked him a lot, but he seemed equally oblivious to that too – all he could see was a ball.

Somewhere else, David thought, he might be having trials

for junior clubs right now. He sighed and felt slightly bad about what he was about to do. But it was the right thing too.

'How's it going, Calvin?' he said. The boy was in his English class but sat at the back and ventured absolutely nothing. As this was a marked improvement from the kids who did nothing but also tried to initiate riots, David had, to his shame, more or less ignored the fact that Calvin turned in no essays, did no prep or reading and seemed entirely content to count down the clock until the second he turned sixteen and he could leave school forever.

This wouldn't have happened at his old school, David thought uncomfortably. They'd have had psychologists and special ed and extra drop-ins and done absolutely everything they could to make sure Calvin could thrive. Here, the fact that he wasn't disruptive was enough for everyone just to leave him alone. He added it to the very long list of things he had to improve.

'Fine,' said Calvin, shooting him a wary look. He'd filled out even more over the summer; his young adolescent gawkiness had gone, his feet looking like huge bananas in white trainers, his neck too long for his thin head. Now his shoulders were broader, his hands huge, his face settling down.

'You look well ... good summer?'

Calvin shrugged.

'Working. Picked fruit.'

'Good for you,' said David, wishing he didn't sound so patronising, when he genuinely meant it. There were lots of fruit-picking jobs available where they didn't ask your age. It was back-breaking outdoor work; David couldn't imagine many Downey boys able to take it on.

Calvin grunted in response.

'So ... GCSEs ...'

David wished he hadn't started that way. GCSEs meant

nothing to a boy like Calvin; he might as well have said astronaut training.

He should have got Mr Craig, the PE teacher, to do this, but he didn't quite see eye to eye with him. Nick Craig couldn't really have a conversation about anything that wasn't sport and the only sport David liked was cricket, which Nicholas didn't consider a real sport at all so their communication was limited. But it was obvious there was something about this boy.

'Listen,' he said finally, abandoning the exam tactic. 'Honestly, I need you to do me a favour.'

Calvin looked at him, squinting.

'I know,' said David. 'But listen. This is embarrassing to ask. But ... do you like singing?'

Calvin kept staring at him.

'What, because I'm black?'

'Oh God, no,' said David, feeling this was going quite badly wrong. 'God no, not that at all.'

'Is this your poncey choir thing?'

'It is,' said David. 'I'm really desperate. Nobody is signing up. And I think ... I think everyone that goes on this thing ... I think it could be really good.'

'What, hanging out with a bunch of snobs? No offence, but no thanks, mate.'

'You could,' said David, eyeing up the ball, 'probably teach them a thing or two.'

'Thought that was your job,' said Calvin, punting it over towards the goal.

'If you sign up, that'll make everyone else do it. People listen to you.'

'Do they?' said Calvin.

'Come off it, you know they do,' said David, and it was so man to man, and not at all teacher to pupil, that Calvin's lips twitched, just a little.

'Why do I want to do it?' said Calvin. 'It's no use to me, man.'

'Aha!' said David. 'Well, I think that's where you're wrong.'

'What do you mean?'

'Well, I can't promise anything,' said David.

And he didn't. But he told him what he'd discussed with Mr Craig. When he'd finished talking, Calvin's large brown eyes had become thoughtful, and the following morning, David saw his name on the sheet, along with the rest of the football team, which, as he'd predicted, brought out the girls en masse, until they were looking at having to hire a spare coach to take them along there.

And David crossed his fingers and hoped to God that he could deliver on his promise.

Chapter Sixteen

Maggie couldn't help it; from relentless nosiness, she was going to find a way to be in the vicinity for their first choir rehearsal. Although it was always, she knew, a mistake to be in the same room as David on school premises. Nobody could concentrate on anything except the two of them, their body language, whether or not they were looking at each other. A year on, they were still the top gossip topic of the entire school. It was a little like being unpleasantly famous.

Nonetheless, she wanted to see it. Mrs Offili was getting out her oldest songs – 'Away in a Manger' and 'The First Nowell' – and working with Dr Fisley, her opposite number at Downey Boys.

Normally they had five choirs – junior boys, with the high alto voices reducing all the grandmothers to tears at the Christmas concert; junior girls; senior boys; senior girls; and a chamber choir, made up of the very best of the boys and girls, which travelled to competitions, and had a justifiably excellent reputation.

For this, however, they'd decided to merge the senior boys and girls – from the third form to the sixth – and do some mixed singing. The senior boys and girls also thought this was rather an excellent idea. The further up the school most of them got, the less appealing a single-sex education appeared to either of them.

Dr Fitzroy and Dr Deveral had, individually, given the choirs short speeches on being inclusive and non-snotty. Alice, an enthusiastic, if supremely ungifted, member of the senior girls, had rolled her eyes and glanced around for Fliss to whisper to, something about why they had to run the proles outreach programme. But, once again, Fliss was standing as far away from her as she possibly could, giving her the total cold shoulder. When was she going to get over this ridiculous pass-agg stance? It was boring and frustrating and most of the other girls, now they'd hit fourth year, had their gangs – the theatre gang, the swots, the pony girls. Alice thought, not for the first time, that she was at the wrong school. She needed to be somewhere with lots of oligarch girls and real money, she knew it.

Fliss hadn't been able to stop, after the first night, her hidden identity. Nothing super abusive that would get her blocked, just the occasional comment – 'yawn' or 'wow huge thighs'. She thought she'd get kicked off. Maybe Alice didn't read them. Which was probably better. Because they made her feel powerful and in control, with no consequences.

David marshalled the troops into the coaches, trying not to betray his nerves. Even going on a coach trip was tricky enough – there weren't any school trips any more, partly because of finance issues and partly because back in the day when they did still have school trips, Phillip Dean had been banned from every country park and museum in the county, repeatedly.

Once all were aboard, shouting, chewing gum, taking pictures with their phones and playing music loudly through their speakers, a habit David would happily have petitioned parliament to make illegal, he swung himself up on the bus, surveyed their faces and smiled.

The kids looked excited, and full of teen bravado, some of the lads with their arms casually slung around the girls. But David saw something under it too: worry. It wasn't their fault. Some of his pupils had rarely or never left the council scheme they'd been born in. Many of them had never even been to Penzance, never mind London or abroad. Their small patch of streets, with graffiti and a park filled with broken glass, was all they had ever known; junkies up Jaybee Avenue, dangerous drunks weaving in and out the small copse of trees. Dogs that couldn't be trusted. People that couldn't be trusted.

'Look,' he said, 'I need to talk to you a bit about this school you're going to.'

The stares ranged from suspicious to actively scowling.

'They can't help it,' he said. 'It's not their fault they were dragged up by nannies and were given so much they can't enjoy anything. A lot of them come from terrible broken homes. They've just never been taught how to behave and they don't know a thing about the real world. Be kind, OK?'

Maggie was giving more or less the same speech back at Downeys. '... it's not their fault, if they seem a little ... rough.'

'I think what you're doing there,' said Isha, 'is denigrating people because their social mores happen to be slightly different from white middle-class norms.'

Maggie bit back that she certainly wasn't middle class, and she grew up eating her dinner at 1 p.m., ta very much.

'Thank you, Isha.'

Isha shrugged, as if all of this should be obvious.

*

72

Inside the bus, rowdy bawdy singing had given way to rather tense nervousness. As the coach turned up the manicured driveway that led to the boys' school there were audible intakes of breath and muttered swears.

'This is a *school*?' said Harrison Fletcher from 4a, although he was so undersized he looked like a first year. 'It looks like a castle.'

'Look at those melts,' said someone else, as they crossed a frosty hockey pitch, where two teams were playing a lively game. Some of the people on the bus laughed, a couple wolf-whistled, but quietly, in case they got into trouble. Some, David noticed, stared with curiosity, even longing.

It felt strange to be coming back to what was, for such a long time, his home. He felt, after the upheaval of the last year, oddly sentimental about it, even more marked when his last house year – then second years, now huge, booming-voiced fourth formers, training for exams – were to be found at the front door, lined up to welcome him.

He smiled as he stepped down and they surrounded him, their easy confidence a contrast to the nerves of the PD crew.

'Hello hello,' he said. 'Who's ready to sing?'

'Are we going to get knifed?' said Ollie Gennell, a blond boy with a beautiful tenor voice. He was half kidding, half, David was astonished to note, genuinely quite nervous about it.

'Don't be ridiculous,' David scoffed. 'And by the way, if I hear the word chav, or the faintest hint of wind-up – I know you wouldn't. But if I did, I'm telling Fitzroy, because I can't have it, OK?'

'Are we allowed to get off with the girls?' asked Richards minor, whose track record in these matters was less than sterling, and who had been looking forward to this for a month.

David knew there was no better way of encouraging boys

73

and girls to get off with one another than completely forbidding them to do it, so he made a half smile and pretended he hadn't understood the question.

James Fisley, the music teacher, was standing waiting for them. He was an incredibly slender, etiolated man, whose nervous sensitivities would probably have done for him in any other school. But here, the boys were protective of him – and impressed by his sensational talent; there was no instrument he couldn't play, no style of music that couldn't flow instantly from his very long fingertips. Too sensitive to be a performer, he had found his niche perfectly in the depths of Cornwall, and Downey's exceptional orchestra was an entire credit to him. If he wasn't quite so nervous, they'd have entered more competitions, but although Dr Fitzroy cajoled him gently every so often, he knew they had a goldmine on their hands and left him to patrol his domain and practice rooms happily, with his head in a world of nothing but pure music.

He made a good match with bullish, confident Mrs Offili from the girls' school, and they balanced one another out very well. But he looked terribly nervous that morning, his long fingers unconsciously flexing and re-flexing under the frayed cuffs of his shirt.

David launched himself back on the bus, where fifty pairs of eyes were staring at him with a mixture of nerves and defiance. 'OK,' he said. 'Let's get our sing on, shall we?' And they filed down after him, almost quiet.

Chapter Seventeen

It was a little, Maggie thought, perched in the balcony seats out of sight, like the Jets and the Sharks in *West Side Story*. Everyone's posture was somewhat wary; the body language challenging and nervous all at once.

The Downey kids in general were taller and thinner than the Phillip Dean kids, and had clearer skin. But the Phillip Dean kids were jokier, more laid-back; the boys and girls, seemingly, more at ease with one another. They were more diverse, less conformist than her girls, with their identically straight flicky hair. There was pink hair, blue; undercuts and earcuffs; trousers so tight that she could barely believe they were school uniform – even thinking this made her immediately feel like Miss Starling.

She saw David's black tousled head below her and felt such a wash of longing for him it blocked out anything she was thinking about the children. Watching him without him knowing she was there – well, watching anyone, she supposed. Watching anyone be good at something – really really good – without them knowing you were watching them. It was incredibly powerful. No wonder rock stars got so many girlfriends. She could watch him all day ...

In the chilly air, Mrs Offili was smiling brightly and shepherding them all in. Pat Carr was often off with stress, for which David couldn't blame her, but nonetheless, it was a sorry sight as he ushered his charges into the large auditorium with its pipe organ, theatre seating, proscenium arch and orchestra pit. Everyone went uncharacteristically quiet.

'OK,' said Mrs Offili, who had grown up in Birmingham and was never intimidated by anyone. 'Do you know what kind of singers you are? Altos, sopranos?'

There was embarrassed mutterings and shuffling of feet. Nobody did.

'Right,' said Mrs Offili, cheerfully. 'Let's get the sorting hat out then.'

And David hid a grin as several of the heads shot up, just for a minute.

Mrs Offili got them all onstage and worked through on the piano – both Downey kids and Phillip Dean kids. The Downey kids knew but it didn't do them any harm to all warm up together, and there was something tribal and binding about being divided into sopranos 1 and 2, altos, baritones. Then there were the three unfortunate basses who were going to have to carry it by themselves: two Downey boys who were both already resigned to the fact that they couldn't ever miss a rehearsal or everything fell apart, and Calvin.

Fliss, already ensconced in the sopranos, wistfully separated from Ismé who sang in the altos, and annoyingly close to the tuneless, yet keen, Alice, glanced over at Calvin, head and shoulders above the other boys. Alice caught her doing it and grinned.

'I thought you were gay now,' she whispered.

'I'm *fluid*,' said Fliss, before she remembered a) that she wasn't talking to Alice and b) she'd just completely given herself away. 'Not that it's anybody's business.'

Alice rolled her eyes. She looked at Calvin more critically.

'Not bad,' she said, examining his tall, lanky body; his casual stance.

'I thought you were still seeing Will,' said Fliss.

'Well, ya,' said Alice thoughtfully. 'But you know. He's in sixth form, he's barely here . . . '

Fliss swallowed down her anger. If she showed anything, any jealousy, any thought at all, Alice would just march in there and take it, just because she could. Alice, so spoilt, so jaded with stuff, never found anything worth having unless somebody else wanted it. Her fingers itched for her phone.

Anyway, thought Fliss, with a rare moment of self-awareness, how likely was it that a hot fourth-former from Phillip Dean was going to be remotely interested in two public schoolgirls? Particularly one with no hair. She grimaced to himself. The pixie cut was growing out. She looked like a rock star from her mother's era. A boy one.

She regarded the two Phillip Dean girls next to her curiously.

'Hey,' she said.

'Hey,' shrugged the one next to her. She was wearing a full face of make-up and dangly earrings. All the Downey girls were scrubbed clean. 'Are you a fourth year?'

'Yeah,' said Fliss indignantly. The two girls exchanged glances and smiles and Fliss wanted to burst into tears.

'Sorry,' said the girl. 'You just look younger.'

'Yeah,' said the other girl, very sarcastically.

Fliss found her lip beginning to wobble. To her absolute surprise Simone leaned over from the altos.

'Well she's not dressed up like she's going to a disco, is she?'

The girls smirked even more.

'What's a "disco"?' said one, making Simone blush puce. She was amazed she'd even managed to defend Fliss in the first place, but the girls reminded her of the kids who'd been

77

mean to her at her own school, and she was finding the entire day very stressful and uncomfortable.

Fliss shot a warning look at Simone, wishing she hadn't interfered and made everything worse.

Thank God, Mrs Offili banged her baton on the top of the piano.

'Right,' she said. 'Now you're sorted. We're going to start singing a round, just to get you all used to it. I'm assuming you all know "London's Burning" and I'll point at your group when it's your turn to come in – I'll be changing it up and down so make sure you're on your toes and paying attention.'

She caught the telltale flash of a screen.

'And I want all phones! Mr McDonald, no phones in Downey House, please. Have you forgotten so quickly?'

'Sorry,' said David, smiling indulgently. He and Mrs Offili had always got on. 'Guys! Put them away! Which means in this box.'

He picked up an empty drawer and his charges all groaned. They were used to Mr McDonald's take on phones, though, and complied with only a few complaints.

'Right,' said Mrs Offili. 'Standing up straight. Taking in deep breaths. Push out your tummies and – SING!'

Maggie had a class, but she came back later and found David standing by the door too, watching them. Mrs Offili had slowly and carefully taught them 'Good King Wenceslas', and goodness me, it was absolutely hair-raising; a tingling sound as the boys roared in with 'Bring me flesh and bring me wine' and the girls replied as the page.

'No way!' said Maggie, delighted. 'Is this working?'

'They're still pretty anxious,' said David, resisting the overwhelming urge to grab her hand and squeeze it. She wasn't even inside the hall. 'But there's something about singing, isn't there?'

'I wouldn't know,' said Maggie, smiling ruefully. 'I sound like a womble when I sing.'

'I like it,' said David.

'When do you ever hear me sing?'

'In the car. You don't know you're doing it. You're like a tiny baby womble.'

'That sounds really annoying,' said Maggie, and David grinned. Then he turned his attention back to the stage.

'I think they're going to be good,' he said. 'It is the best thing – when you're singing it pushes all the other stuff out of your head, doesn't it? You can't really focus on anything else.'

Maggie thought how when David was focusing on his job he rarely noticed anything else, but didn't mention it.

'They're wonderful,' she said. 'They're going to be great.' That was about fifteen seconds before the fight broke out.

The part singing was where it all fell down. Downey kids had been trained to sing in harmony, Phillip Dean kids only in unison, and the difficulty of singing something different to what you were hearing was making them nervous and fidgety.

Dr Fisley had tried to mix the two groups in together as much as possible so they could follow the home singers, but what was happening was the Phillip Dean kids, particularly the boys, were either falling silent or launching in and getting it terribly wrong, drawing looks from the local boys that they interpreted as hostile or jeering. 'Once in Royal David's City' fell apart extremely quickly and the entire thing ground to a halt.

One of the Downey boys, meaning well, suggested something simpler, like 'Away in a Manger', and one of the PD boys shot back, 'What, like for little kids,' and there was, all of a sudden, a tension in the air.

It had, on balance, been going too well for too long. Then there had been a bit of a scuffle at the back of the baritones. One of the alto singers had come in at the wrong time – a pretty, buxom girl called Kelisa Davidson – and a couple of the Downey Boys, including Richards minor, had sniggered and nudged each other and said something along the lines of how they wouldn't mind coming in early, or some normal boy nonsense, not realising, as only boys who went to single-sex schools could be so stupid, that Kelisa's half-brother Archie Silver, who'd been held back two years and thus was nearly eighteen years old and looked like – and indeed dreamed of becoming – a cage fighter, happened to be standing right behind them.

The Downey boys had done a little light boxing as part of the schools sports teams. Silver, on the other hand, had actually been in fights. He knew that you didn't mention you were going to fight, you didn't call someone out for a fight, you didn't bounce around people on the soles of your feet or tell them to come ahead and have a go if they thought you were hard enough.

You just whacked them as hard as you could somewhere you knew it would really really hurt – in this case, one of the boys' kidneys – then got as far away as you could as quickly as possible.

By the time the uproar had subsided and the outraged shouting had stopped – Mr Fisley being useless, Mrs Offili and David doing the bulk of the heavy lifting – the two sets of boys were apart, staring at one another, and there was a tense atmosphere in the room, hissing insults being traded, until the pushing started. For a moment it looked like they might have a riot on their hands.

'Right, CALM DOWN,' said David, his voice surprisingly loud and commanding, testament to his military genes. 'Now listen,' he continued, addressing both sides, 'we're not going to have any of this stuff between us.'

'They're calling our girls slags!' said one of the Phillip Dean boys.

'Oi!' said the girls.

'Well, they shouldn't dress like slags then,' said Richards minor, who really was a manifest idiot. The whole room went quiet at this. David was suddenly incandescent with fury. He drew himself up to his full height – there were few people taller than him in the school – and summoned the boy out.

'I am not,' he said through gritted teeth, 'going to embarrass you in front of the entire school, because I disapprove of that. But you will go straight to Dr Fitzroy's office and sit outside it until I come and find you.'

'You don't work here,' said the boy, his blond hair and bright blue eyes turning hard and entitled.

There was a further silence. Then to everyone's surprise, meek Dr Fisley stepped up.

'No,' he said, his timid voice quavering, 'but I do. And you don't dare talk like that to anyone or about anyone. And if Dr Fitzroy doesn't rusticate you for this I'll find something he will rusticate you for. Now. OUT!'

Everyone fell silent at this uncharacteristic display of backbone from the mild-mannered teacher. He turned round to address them all, glancing at David, who gave him the thumbs up and nodded in thanks.

'Listen,' Dr Fisley went on, 'I can only apologise for any disrespectful behaviour. And hope that you can too. But it doesn't matter. Because we're just here for the music. And music doesn't care who you are or where you come from. In here, it's only this. I know it's difficult. Beautiful stuff is usually quite hard, OK? But we still think it's best if we all sing together and help one another. All right? Or we can just call this off right now and I'll get Mr McDonald to take you home.'

The dining hall wasn't far away from the auditorium, and already the delicious smell of home-made lasagne was drifting through. People fidgeted anxiously but nobody piped up again.

'OK,' said Dr Fisley. 'We're going to do the song we did last year. It's Scottish but please don't feel you have to do the accent. There's no harmony until the end, but it will be beautiful if we do it or not. Do you understand? I'm splitting you all up now, you're going into different rooms and we'll try it this afternoon. I'll be wanting to see which one of the groups can step up to the mark.'

Nobody could help feeling a bit of a failure. The whole idea of the two year groups blending in harmony had lasted just slightly less than thirty-five minutes, and now they were more or less to be shut away into locked rooms to keep them apart, however much Dr Fisley tried to pretend this was something they'd planned all along.

In each of the rooms the children, separated from one another, got their heads down, intimidated by the beautiful instruments and the tall old rooms, the windows looking out either onto the wonderfully tended frosted grounds, or over the wild sea beyond.

'This is all snobs, innit,' said Kelisa, shaking off the insult, but even she was soon caught up in the demanding and thorough lesson, as they each learned the simple melodic line, then practised it over and over again until it was perfect. This wasn't the usual Phillip Dean method of doing things, and the children were surprised how relentless it was. But they took to it with gusto, and it felt like no time at all before the bell rang for lunch, and the children looked up, amazed.

Lunchtime looked like apartheid, thought David, surveying the long benches where the two schools huddled apart, staring at each other. The Downey boys and girls weren't even sitting together. It seemed sad.

In fact, it was anything but.

The Downey girls were having a massive conversation – except for Ismé who, predictably, had gone and sat with the Phillip Dean girls, particularly the girls, who eye-rolled to each other, as did the Downey girls. Immediately. 'So,' she began, 'everyone read Reni Eddo-Lodge?'

Back at the Downey table, talk was entirely of the boys. Calvin was mentioned more than once, as was Archie Silver and several other boys – out of uniform, or rather, anything Downey House would class a uniform, with hair long, dyed; with home-made tattoos disfiguring arms already, these boys were incredibly exotic and dangerous, i.e., catnip to a bunch of girls locked up in an all-girls' boarding school. Maggie sat and ate at the same table pretending to be ignoring them but in fact listening intently.

One thing heartily appreciated by almost everyone was the food – hearty lasagnes, meat and vegetarian, garlic bread, followed by mince pies and cream. The fare at Phillip Dean was shopped in from frozen. There was general appreciation in the room. Silence descended as the last of the mince pies was eaten, and David took his cue.

'OK,' he said. 'Half an hour of lunchtime left. Anyone want a kickabout?'

Chapter Eighteen

Outside it was cold, but bright, the sun low in the sky, getting in people's eyes. Frost still crackled on the playing fields but it didn't bother the boys, as they burst out onto the grounds, desperate to get rid of some built-up energy and tension. The girls, cooler, sauntered out behind them, none of them admitting they might want a game too.

As soon as the game started it became clear that the Downey boys might look taller, but the Phillip Dean boys knew their way around a football field. They played fast and furious, automatically deferring to Calvin, their natural captain. The Downey boys didn't know what hit them, and they were three–nil down before the bell rang.

David had quietly fetched Nicholas Craig, head of PE. The two men had never been particular friends in the common room, Nicholas thinking David's total ignorance of all sport except cricket was a fey pretension; David not thinking about Nicholas at all, ever, but they respected one another and David had asked him to come down and take a look at Calvin.

Of course scouts came down to Exeter, and Calvin had been spotted in various street games. But there were a lot – a lot – of extremely talented boys, who wanted little more than the chance to play professional football; who saw it as their way out. He'd had a trial with the juniors, but made it no further so far, and he had no parents at home pushing him on, making him take extra training. He had natural talent and the streets, and that wasn't enough.

Nicholas, on the other hand, was leaning forwards, watching intently.

'He thinks it's over for him with football,' said David, his arms folded against the cold as Calvin expertly lobbed another goal into the corner of the net, as fast as if it had been fired from a gun. 'He's nearly sixteen. He's getting too old.'

'Hmm,' said Nicholas, as Calvin effortlessly zipped past the entire defence line, dancing with his feet. 'But you know, the lottery selectors ...'

David shook his head, he didn't know.

'Well, they're looking for gold medals, so they'll funnel you into other sports if they can. And his physique ...'

Nicholas carried on watching him.

'He's just so fast, and his feet are brilliant,' he said and David pretended to nod as if in agreement with an opinion he had independently come to.

'I'd like to see him in field hockey,' said Nicholas, tapping his mouth with his fingers. 'He's got control too ... in a less crowded field than football ... God. He'd stand out a mile ...'

David blinked.

'I did wonder.'

Nicholas looked at him.

'Is he academic?'

'I don't know.'

'Well, you're his teacher, aren't you?'

David nodded. 'Yes, but ... well. I mean. No. But potentially ... I'm not sure. Difficult background.'

'I'd need to see him in action,' said Nicholas. 'But he could ... yeah. He really could help us out. With a few things, I wouldn't wonder.'

David nodded. The cups and medals that lined the beautifully outfitted sports department testified to how seriously Nicholas took competition, even if he was looking casual now, standing in the cold in his tracksuit as if it didn't affect him, which it probably didn't.

'So is it worth a shot, do you think?'

'I'd love him,' said Nicholas, without hesitation. 'But he'd have to pass his GCSEs.'

Calvin shot home a beautiful goal, the entire groups of the two schools cheered; it was so effortlessly done.

'Yup, given half a chance at the scholarship, I'd love him,' said Nicholas, turning round. 'But I have a feeling the hard work is down to you.'

Chapter Nineteen

Another hour's separate rehearsal after lunch, and then at the end of the school day they were led out to close a special assembly.

Dr Fitzroy read out a speech of welcome that was rather less pompous than his normal standard and actually rather appreciated. They also looked extremely nervous; pale in fact, standing at the back of the huge stage in front of everyone. Dr Fisley, who had Mrs Offili to accompany them very gently at the grand piano, was standing in front of them with a conductor's baton.

'And now,' he said, 'we are going to perform a song half of us had never heard this morning.'

The school clapped politely. Alice rolled her eyes.

The piano was so soft it was almost inaudible, and the tune it played was like a lullaby. And gently the first voices came in, all in unison, but incredibly quiet.

'This day to you is born a child ... '

Dr Fisley had chosen very well; all the parts were in unison until the end, and very very quiet, which was forgiving to the nervous and the new. But the song itself was beautiful.

'Of Mary meek, the Virgin mild ... that blessed bairn ... '

Maggie was and always had been a wreck with this carol, and seeing the two schools – the spots, the awkwardness, the swagger – hearing the different voices, to see it all shrugged off in gentle song, the gawkiness of the hulking boys, the pouting girls, the make-up and the awkward shapes shaved into eyebrows and hair, the smell of Lynx and Beyoncé perfume and nerves and the desperation of being so very nearly sixteen . . . it all fell away. Leaving only the sweet, soft purity of eighty young voices singing a soft lullaby to the infant birth.

'Balooo, lammy, balulalow,' whispered the rocking voices. Maggie noticed she wasn't the only teacher there hiding their face or discreetly wiping their eyes. She glanced at David, who felt it instantly, and, when he tried to shoot her the most secret of glances, keeping her hands tight to her sides, she nonetheless gave him a massive, bracing thumbs up.

'Baloo, lammy, balulalow.'

CHRISTMAS

Chapter Twenty

The problem was, finding time and space to be together was still extremely difficult. Maggie was on watch several nights a week and couldn't leave. David was at full stretch trying to compensate for a decade of poor schooling for his year elevens before they sat their exams. Both of them were flooded with marking.

And those thirty miles of winding country roads in the dark that separated them were not for the faint-hearted. David's flat was plain and miserable – he hadn't thought about it for a second when he'd rented it, full of despair after the break-up with Miranda, his ex-fiancée, and it felt like it. There was a formica kitchen left over from the sixties, and a saggy, sad old bed that felt like loads of people had died in it.

And of course he couldn't come to Maggie's. And they couldn't keep spending money on hotels, that was impossible and ridiculous and impractical. But moving in together ... they were nowhere near ready; nowhere near.

And now Christmas was looming, but Maggie was already feeling the pressure from home. Stan was back at his parents', recuperating, and Anne was banging on at her for when she was coming, and could she look after Cody and Dylan for a night or two, give Mum a break, give her a break. There still hung over everything a sense of blame.

'I thought . . . ' David had said, 'my friend Cornelius does this thing in Somerset . . .'

'You have a friend called Cornelius?'

'You have a friend called Jambo McGloag; I've seen them in your phone.'

Maggie screwed up her face.

' . . . anyway, the whole village performs the nativity outside. There's hundred of them. There's animals and stuff. I mean, it's usually freezing, but it doesn't matter if you believe or not, it's really special and I wondered if you'd like to go . . . '

'I would,' said Maggie. 'But . . . my family want me home.'

David put his hands up.

'You're kidding.'

'It's Christmas!' said Maggie. 'I always go home at Christmas . . . and this year . . .'

David shook his head.

'Right. OK.'

'I'm sorry,' said Maggie. 'I can't . . . it's delicate. I don't want to fall out with my family because of you.'

'They haven't even met me,' said David, a trifle shortly, which wasn't like him.

Maggie swallowed.

'Well,' she said, 'that's what I was thinking. Why don't you come with me?'

David looked nervous.

'You could . . . maybe stay somewhere else? Maybe we could get somewhere? And I could . . . '

'Introduce me slowly?'

Maggie walked up to him. She came up to his chest, and held him, looking straight up into his dark eyes.

'I think you're awesome,' she said, slowly and carefully. 'And I love them. And therefore, they'll love you too.'

*

It had not turned out like that.

Christmas had been awkward. Maggie had felt out of place as soon as she'd got back. She would have expected, with Stan on the mend, that he would fade out of her family's life. That was normally what happened with exes, wasn't it?

But somehow he was there all the time every day, still calling her mum Mrs Adair, sitting in the same chair at the dining table. He was back at work but they'd put him in the back office and it seemed to be suiting him well, even if paper distribution wasn't what it was. Anne would be sitting next to him and laughing at his stories and it genuinely felt to Maggie as if they'd chosen him over her.

She'd considered whether Anne could possibly be after him, but of course she couldn't. Anne had always had the highest levels of integrity; was fiercely proud of her boys and her hair salon and her immaculate house and was generally disapproving of Maggie deserting everyone. She took the boys to mass. The idea of her stealing her sister's ex was simply not possible, and she, Maggie, was being paranoid. Stan had been through a terrible time. Nonetheless she quietly had a word with her mother to make sure that Stan would be otherwise engaged when David arrived for a two-day stay (at a local bed and breakfast – it wasn't at all nice, but it was hard to find anything at Christmas time at short notice), seeing as the last time the two men had met, Stan had taken a swing at David and David had probably deserved it.

Also, she realised crossly – and she was extremely annoyed with herself for doing so – she was looking through new eyes at their little ex-council house her father had proudly bought, and seeing it as rather common, accustomed as she was to the pared-back taste of Downey House – the squeaky white leather three-piece suite, the net curtains, the wooden 'farmhouse' kitchen.

It was absurd, she knew, and she adored her parents, but the flat she and Stan had shared had had sleek IKEA lines and plain decor, and although she hadn't met David's family, she knew his father was a retired colonel; his brother a commander in the navy. She was angry that of course David wouldn't mind – her family were decent people, who cared if they still had old orange carpeting on the stairs and huge framed school pictures of Maggie and Anne on the wall, toothless?

It was making her irritated and edgy. The plan was he'd spend a couple of days at hers and then they'd go visit his dad, but, of course, what they desperately actually needed was time, the two of them, on their own. It was like having to cope with in-laws before they were even boyfriend and girlfriend. But her mother's voice when she'd suggested missing a Christmas had been unbearable.

David, though, did his best not to show any nerves, bounding in at the door with a large bouquet of flowers and two bottles of good red wine that her father regarded with suspicion, as if David was challenging him to some kind of competition.

'Oh yes, a Male-bec,' he said, as if he knew what it was, making Maggie wince then hate herself for wincing, particularly when it became clear that Anne had noticed her do it.

'He's very handsome,' whispered her mother in the kitchen, which was true, obviously, but it felt rather as if her mother was trying to be understanding about her choices; as if she'd been so carried away she couldn't be expected to help herself.

Maggie smiled tightly and took in the plates to set the dining table they rarely used. David jumped up, hitting his head on the overhead light, offering to help. Maggie's dad gave him a look.

'Naw, you're all right,' he said shortly, as if David was showing him up by even asking. Maggie couldn't blame him, not really – he and Stan had been going to Celtic matches together for years before his daughter had inexplicably thrown out the window all his plans for taking his grand-children too, like he did with Cody and Dylan, like he had with his siblings; good west coast Catholics who lived near each other, who had Sunday lunch with their families and were in and out of each other's lives.

It was the only life he'd ever known and this stranger was messing with it and he felt he had a right to feel slightly grumpy: to be polite would be disloyal to the man he thought of as his son-in-law, whether they'd gone through with it or not.

Maggie's mum knew all this and shot him a cross look.

'So, tell me about being an English teacher,' she said. 'Why did you want to do that? It's quite unusual for a man, isn't it?'

'Not really,' said David, trying to smile politely. 'Maybe in English it is more, but I just always loved books and read-ing, and I want to be in teaching – teachers helped me a lot growing up.'

'Yeah, sounds like a girls' job,' said Maggie's dad in a fake friendly manner, and Maggie wanted to kick him under the table.

'I like the immediacy of it all. There's no zoning out, or switching off, or checking your phone. You have to be there all the time, with these young minds – they can be tricky, or funny, but they're always interesting. I know teachers com-plain a lot but actually it's got really high job satisfaction, teaching.'

'Well, I know our Maggie's always loved it,' said her mum proudly.

'She's very good at it,' said David promptly, at which

her father rolled his eyes and Maggie wanted to throw a cup at him.

'This is lovely cottage pie,' said David, realising he was laying it on far too thick but completely not sure what the correct thing to do was. Maggie had gone very pink, her cheeks clashing with her red hair, and he desperately wanted to make things better but it felt like the more he tried the more stilted he became.

'It's shepherd's pie,' grunted her father.

There was silence.

'Uhm, OK,' said David, completely unaware what he'd done wrong now, and Maggie was hot and red, absolutely furious at everyone without being able to articulate why.

'So, have you been watching the cricket?' asked David eventually, trying to find some common ground.

Maggie's dad sniffed.

'The *what*?' he said incredulously.

'Dad!' protested Maggie.

'What?' said her dad. 'Who watches the cricket?'

'Loads of people!'

'Aye, English people!'

'I'm sorry,' said David.

'Don't apologise!' said Maggie. 'Dad, you're being *so* rude.'

'Oh, I'm being *"so rude"* am I,' grumbled her father, mimicking a posh English accent. 'Oh, I'm most terribly, terribly sorry! Frightfully!'

'Jim,' said her mother, reprovingly, but Maggie, watched closely by Anne, had already got up.

'Actually,' she said, trembling, realising once she was up she didn't quite know what she was going to do – in the past she'd have slammed her way out of the house, but she wasn't a teenager any more arguing about politics. She was an adult, introducing them to the most important man in her life, the most important man she'd ever met, who was currently staring at a plate of either cottage or shepherd's pie, his ears burning. Oh, for heaven's sake. The rest of the room was looking at her curiously.

'Uhm, I'll just go check in the kitchen,' she said wildly, needing to grab a chance to calm herself down. Ninety seconds, she reminded herself, from something she'd read about trying to control her temper (after an outburst or two in class she hadn't been particularly proud of).

Ninety seconds. That's all I need. Ninety seconds to calm down.

She stood over the sink, trying to breathe carefully, as her mother came into the little kitchen and shut the door behind her.

She stood next to her, gently caressing Maggie's red curls.

'He's nice,' she said, quietly, in that comforting way she had. 'He's nice. That's why your da is acting up. He's threatened. He hoped ... we all ... well. He hoped this might be a passing thing. Just a bit of foolishness. But he can see it isn't. He can see you mean it this time. That you're going to leave us for this man, and move down south and have English babies ... '

Her voice cracked. Maggie turned round, even though her heart leapt at the very idea, and took her mother in her arms.

'It's just down the road,' she said.

'Edinburgh is just down the road!' said her mum. 'Falkirk! Dundee! Stirling! There are plenty of men there! Plenty of posh schools! Cornwall ... '

Maggie never saw her staunch mother cry, not even when she'd called off her wedding.

'This is forever. You mean it,' said her mum. 'And I'm losing you.'

'You've got Anne,' said Maggie. 'I've been away for ages! You've already got used to it!'

Her mother pulled back and looked up into Maggie's face.

'I'm a mother,' she said fiercely. 'Of course I don't bloody get used to it.'

Chapter Twenty-one

It would be nice to say that visiting David's family went better, but that would be something of a stretch.

They were uncomfortable on the long drive down to Dorset; the roads were jammed full of happy-looking families with presents piled high up on their back seats; pink-cheeked children and cars loaded with skis.

Even choosing what to buy one another had been a minefield, seeing as it was such a new relationship. Maggie had bought David an early-edition Wordsworth, which she realised quickly he already had, and he had bought her a cherry-coloured cloche, which she loved, obviously, but had thought maybe he'd get her ... Stan had always bought her a charm for the charm bracelet she had now not worn in a very long time. It had been easy and sweet and suited them both. She wasn't exactly sure what to do with a cloche.

David's father still walked like the soldier he'd once been. The house, a beautiful rambling old manse in the country, was immaculately neat and tidy, everything squared away. There were well-dusted pictures of men in uniforms covering every inch of the dark red walls – relatives, platoons, groups of young men everywhere. Maggie couldn't see David in any of them, but recognised plenty of his brother in his naval uniform. There were also very pretty pictures of his mother on her wedding day and holding each of the boys.

'You're her double,' said Maggie, wonderingly, staring at them for a long time. David smiled sadly. 'Yes, people say that. Murdo's more like Dad really.'

Murdo was on manoeuvres in the North Atlantic but it was a matter of some excitement when they managed, briefly, to raise him on a very bad Skype connection. His gruff tones didn't sound like his brother at all, but there was a very clear warmth in his tone when he saw them all together.

'A wee Scottish lass,' David's father was saying. He was very proud of some distant Scottish heritage, hence Murdo. 'Och aye the noo.' Maggie smiled the best she could and tried to look nonchalant, even when David's father asked him how Miranda, his ex, was bearing up.

'She's fine,' said David shortly, which Maggie, who happened to know she was not remotely fine, simply brushed over.

After a plain supper of mince and potatoes, the house went to bed promptly at 9 p.m.; Maggie was in a small room that would once have belonged to the servants, she was guessing. She considered getting up and creeping out to where David was but she didn't want to freak the colonel out if she ran into him unexpectedly, particularly not on her very first time of meeting him. She rather thought David might come to her, but he didn't.

They weren't able to feel themselves again, truly, till they got back to Cornwall, leaving early – the colonel did everything early – and beating the traffic, the cold winter sun taking forever to rise against the empty frost-tipped fields; the winding roads of Cornwall welcoming them back again, bare trees looming up either side.

Staring out of the window on the passenger side, Maggie saw a huge hare, pinging across a white field like a kangaroo. He looked ecstatically fast and free and she stared at him somewhat enviously as he vanished straight over a barbed wire fence. She bet he hadn't just spent the Christmas holidays trying to get on with your new boyfriend's family when you'd barely dated him anyway so nobody even knew if you were jumping ahead of yourself. Putting all your eggs in one basket didn't even begin to cover it.

However, back at Reuben's – where the staff clearly thought they were having an affair – it was different. The place was deserted, the summer surfers gone, and they had their pick of the rooms overlooking the sea. It was freezing and grey out there, but warm and cosy indoors, and with an absolute yelp of relief, they both crawled into bed after lunch and made up for lost time, and Christmas was saved, more or less, in the special place between all the demands of school and family and the world beyond their bubble; even if that place suddenly seemed very small, a little fragile.

SPRING TERM

Chapter Twenty-two

For Maggie, the very first thing on the agenda with her home class was the stress of their mock GCSEs. From day one, they all looked absolutely terrified, apart from Alice Trebizon-Woods, who was doing her best to look like she didn't care, or perhaps genuinely didn't. Most terrified of all was Simone, which was ridiculous seeing as she was top of the class for pretty much everything. She also looked pale and unwell, as if she'd spent the entire break stuck inside a stuffy room study-ing and having pastries shoved down her throat every ten minutes, which was more or less what had in fact happened.

Fliss was absolutely furious because Hetty had got a car – a car! – for Christmas. 'We can trust you,' her mother had said, loudly, in Fliss's earshot. 'We know you'll be respon-sible, darling, and you've worked so hard for it.'

'You'll never get a car,' Hattie had hissed later. 'And you're not coming in mine either.'

'Who wants to get crashed in your stupid car?' said Fliss, furiously. '*And* it's only a Fiat. I wouldn't even tell my friends I had a Fiat, I'd be too embarrassed.'

'Well lucky for you you won't have to then,' said Hattie, and had then proceeded to drive back to school without her.

Fliss had vanished back into the online world of Seo-Joon. The character had seemed real to her; she liked posts of bubble tea, of k-pop stars, of Korean accounts she couldn't even read. Meanwhile, she left little notes here and there. 'Ugh, boring' on a picture of Alice's Mauritius diving expedition. 'Yuk' on a picture of Will. It was addictive and so thrilling. She followed Calvin from Phillip Dean, but he never posted at all. If Calvin had ever thought about his image he might have done; he had no embarrassment at all about spending Christmas Day with his grandmother and several neighbourhood 'aunties' who brought food and music, if not terribly expensive gifts, and they had all had a very jolly time altogether.

Back at school, they had two weeks before the exams began, and the cracks started to show almost immediately. Fliss was fussing while Simone desperately tried to placate her; Alice became lazier and more worldly wise than ever while Ismé did more eye-rolling and complaining than was normal even for a fifteen-year-old girl.

The rest of the class was equally stressed, and Maggie was catching it. They were as well prepared and motivated as any collection of pupils could ever be. The school bent over backwards to take a personal interest in each and every one of them; to help them on their way, to do their absolute best. All of the teachers were effectively on call 24/7; no problem was considered too small to be taken seriously and talked through. Ismé was threatening not to sit them at all unless they decolonised the curriculum, which would put her scholarship at risk and had been met with implacable opposition by Miss Starling, traditionalist head of the department. It was wearying.

'They have everything,' Maggie complained to David. 'We had nothing. I don't think my parents even knew when my exam was. I was just sent out to get on with it. And these are only their prelims! Mocks.'

David went quiet. After his mother had died he had hidden himself in the school library; kept away from the well-meaning buffoonery, the casual punch or arm round the shoulders that were all his fellow boys could do to express their sympathy. The librarian had been an old, rather dried-up character, nearing retirement, and she kept her counsel but fed him novel after novel throughout the cheerlessness of the next two years. When the exams came up he flew through them without even noticing them; he'd never done so much as a past paper.

But now he could do with a bit of Maggie's spoonfeeding for his own kids. There was a general defeatist attitude, coupled with the rather more lax approach to absenteeism throughout exam time. Only 8 per cent of the children at Phillip Dean scraped three A levels; 92 per cent of Downey House kids did. It was insane.

'You're miles away,' said Maggie. They were walking David's dog Stephen Dedalus across the frozen cliffs above the sea. It was a glorious Cornish winter's day, and they had headed south, away from any possible prying eyes, even if what most of the children had in mind for this weekend was huddling as close to the radiators in the common rooms as possible, ideally while getting away with wearing fluffy pyjamas all day in the name of studying. Maggie had been trying to strongly push the message of *The Scarlet Letter* all year. From the ongoing froideur between Fliss and her dorm mates (she hadn't managed to swap dorms), she wasn't a hundred per cent sure it was getting across.

'Just thinking,' said David, throwing a stick for Stephen Dedalus, who was already the happiest dog in the world, and only became more so bouncing along the cracking grass, examining his paws in surprise when he hit a puddle and cracked through the thin layer of rime.

'Just an idea,' he said, eventually. 'I suck at exam prep.'

Maggie grinned at him affectionately. 'You don't suck at anything,' she said. 'It's just because you think they should all love the source material as much as you do so they shouldn't need it.'

'Well, whatever,' said David. 'It just seems so box-ticky.'

'Welcome to teaching.'

'Yes, but ... you know what I mean. But also I always think the best way to understand something is to discuss it, to explain it ...'

'Mmm,' said Maggie.

'Why don't we get the kids out and about? Get them to come to us, talk about the books – they're all doing the same ones.'

They were. *The Tempest* and *Great Expectations*. Maggie and David had cooked it up between them as their favourite of each of the choices on offer.

'*Great Expectations* could be a good debate,' mused Maggie. 'About winning the lottery?'

David nodded. 'I think so.'

'What if they all end up falling out and shouting and it goes all pear-shaped?'

'It will still get them thinking about it. As a living work; as something relevant to them,' said David.

Maggie smiled at him.

'You're clever,' she said, grinning.

'I know,' said David, wrinkling his nose. 'Pointless, isn't it?'

Maggie glanced at her watch.

'Is it time for a bun?'

'Yup.'

'Well then. You've earned a bun.'

Chapter Twenty-three

Miss Starling had sniffed and predicted dire outcomes for what Maggie had boldly decided to call the 'conference' but was overruled by Maggie pointing out what their commitment was to Phillip Dean, and how much this would cover it.

The fourth years were excited and anxious, and desperate for a change of scene; the weather had turned grey and miserable and everywhere there was low-hanging anxiety about the weight of the exams ahead.

Also, the appeal of the Phillip Dean boys – not just rangy Calvin; there were plenty of dangerous bad boys, compared to the clean-cut Ben Fogle style of their Downey House counterparts – was not to be understated.

More than a few Downey girls went to bed the night before with visions of them somehow saving Calvin in the manner of the heiress who married the extremely attractive fugitive and went to live on a yacht for the rest of their lives. There was a positively daring amount of lip gloss and some unusually heavy brows getting groomed on the coach on the way there. Maggie chose to ignore it. She didn't really care why they were engaging, just that they did. And David was right. You needed to give context to a piece which was more than just rehashing the same essays time and time over, learning quotes until they became meaningless, or simply filling in the things examiners were looking for without reflecting, at least once, on how the work moved you, how it made you feel and expanded your horizons; that it wasn't just a dead weight you had to carry around before you expelled it on the exam paper and never thought about it again.

She looked at their faces as they entered the rusting school gates. There was barbed wire everywhere, and a special locked section for teachers' cars. There were high entrance gates at the front door, if pupils ever needed to be searched, and most of the doors were on constant lockdown.

Cigarette butts and crisp packets littered the area – however much David tried to engage his litter patrol, it never quite went away forever – and the placing of the school at the dead end of town meant the pitiful grounds were raked with harsh sea winds from the depressed waterfront. Cracked window panes patched with cardboard and broken concrete steps completed the picture. The girls went quiet, a little nervous, some of them. Ismé, on the contrary, got louder.

'Oh, a bit of real actual life,' she was saying loudly, filming it on her mobile phone. 'You lot aren't going to know what hit you.'

'Maybe,' said Alice tartly, 'it'll just be a bunch of people with ideas like us? I don't know, just a thought.'

For once, Maggie was happy at Alice's blunt manner. Ismé, as usual, rolled her eyes.

Simone, on the other hand, was terrified. She thought that people were looking at her, judging her for coming from this sort of background. And the people in the school, they were going to hate her just like the kids at her old school had. She didn't fit in anywhere, she thought, sighing. Every time she got a chance to feel like she might, everything went to crap again and she knew she wasn't part of anyone's world; she had left her old orbit so far behind but the new orbit didn't suit her. Obviously if she'd looked like beautiful Ismé, she could go and do whatever she wanted. That was what was worse, she thought. It wasn't rich and poor. It was pretty and cool, and non pretty and uncool, and the pretty ones didn't even realise how easily they excluded her or thought she didn't matter.

David had commandeered the dining hall stroke gym hall, which stank of feet and macaroni cheese all in a oner, because the windows had had to be replaced on the cheap and now they didn't open and the place always smelled absolutely awful.

Maggie glared at her classes fiercely as they entered, but that had absolutely no effect on Alice, who wrinkled her perfect little button nose the tiniest fraction as they headed in.

David's year elevens were already seated, glowering. As if they needed a bunch of snobs coming in to tell them how stupid they were. Calvin was sitting near the back as ever, but slightly more alert. David watched him closely. He'd tried to impress on him how important this was but as usual had absolutely no idea if he was getting through to him. He'd suggested to him that he have a word with his grandmother but Calvin had simply laughed. His grandmother had left school when she was nine years old. Still – he was present, which was something, and leaning forwards, which wasn't nothing.

Interestingly, Maggie thought, although it was a matter of gossipy interest to the Downey students, the Phillip Dean students clearly couldn't care less that they were a couple. She found this oddly reassuring, even as she still avoided David's eye and tried not to smile too much in his general direction, or watch him as he took the centre of the room.

'Welcome, Downey House, to Phillip Dean,' he said.

Someone sniffed theatrically but he carried on and ignored it.

'We're going to do a joint dissection – I'll be dividing you into small working parties, and we'll be looking for short presentations on the following sections of *Great Expectations*. Dress, historical context, major themes.'

'Whether Pip gets nobbed,' said Archie Silver, to an outburst of boyish sniggering.

'If you're engaging that much,' said David, 'yes, you can talk about the realism of their love affair. You can talk about the alternative ending and whether that would work better.'

'Well, obviously it would, because in the end Estella couldn't really give two shits for him because he's poor,' said Ismé.

Fliss stood up hotly, looking straight at Calvin.

'That's crap,' she said. 'That's nonsense. If she really loved him, it doesn't matter.'

'Only people with money ever say that it doesn't matter,' said Ismé. 'It doesn't happen, all these ups and downs.'

'But Dickens thought it did,' said Maggie, smiling. 'He thought you could. In a much more separated segregated society than ours. Just like Cinderella or any other fairy story.'

'*Pretty Woman*,' said someone else.

'Good example,' said Maggie automatically.

'But it doesn't happen!' said Ismé, glaring at her.

Calvin, of all people, laughed softly from the back.

'You're the one getting on the bus back to the castle,' he said in his deep voice.

Fliss felt the familiar burst of terrible jealousy but she wasn't sure which of the two it was directed towards.

'Good,' said David, pleased. 'You do have to think about whether it is possible, as it was for Pip, or whether it's a self-fulfilling prophecy that you can't.'

'Everything's stacked against you,' said Ismé.

David nodded.

'Well, you still live in a free country, in a rich part of the world,' someone snorted.

'I know, I know. But I'm just telling you. It's not all stacked against you. We will never know how many Einsteins and Mozarts we lost to the sweatshops and the plantations. But Dickens did not believe it always had to be that way. It wasn't for him, and it needn't be for you.'

And he was staring straight at Calvin as he said it.

Maggie had been right; it had been good for them to mix things up a bit, think about their work differently. Or, in half of her class's heads, think relentlessly about Calvin, recast him as Pip and dream of being his Estella. Which was also, Maggie decided, absolutely fine. It would add passion to their writing, their arguments and quite possibly their personal essays.

She counted them all onto the coach, took them back to school, showed Miss Starling nobody had got into trouble, made sure they all entered the dinner hall, then got back into her little car and drove the thirty miles straight down the road again.

David grinned to see her.

'Seriously. You cannot possibly get that turned on by standing in the Phillip Dean assembly hall all day.'

'You,' she said, smothering him in kisses, 'would be amazed.'

The weather stayed bleak as the exams wore on, with tears, fraught fights over library books, late-night meltdowns – and this was only the mocks, Maggie thought wearily. But eventually they were through the long days; the dusty, hot examination hall in one of the gymnasiums, long, immaculate rows of desks; a huge clock ticking noisily overhead;

the sound of scuffling; of frantic rubbing out and the slow, patient walk of an invigilator up and down the aisles of desks, watching for furtive glances up sleeves for quotes or the flash of a phone, even though everything had been locked away before the examination hall had been opened.

It was funny; although you had to concentrate, Maggie had always rather enjoyed invigilating. It was a simple task-focused structure of handing out extra sheets of paper and collecting in early returned papers – some for better, ticked and smug; some for worse, tear-stained or scribbled upon or simply mostly blank, although there were fewer of those here than at her old school. It reminded her a little of church; silence and ritual and, for once in the loud noisy shouty life of the school, a little quiet and peace among the rushing of the day.

Of course it wouldn't feel like that on the other side of the desk. But Maggie had been one of those people who had enjoyed exams; the feeling of being pent-up, stuffed full of knowledge, ready to put it down precisely, with new sta-tionery; had loved the challenge of the creative essay or the multiple choice quiz. And even now she could see some of her pupils diligently concentrating, writing quickly, glancing regularly at the clock.

Please let them do all right, she said to herself. She wouldn't be allowed to invigilate the real exams when the time came, so it was a good chance to watch them in action, see how they reacted under pressure. Simone was writing screeds, far too much, and needed help, perhaps, to streamline her thoughts. Alice was sighing and glancing round as if to show how bored she was. Poor Alice, thought Maggie for the first time. She was probably destined to live a performative life – the holidays, the sports cars, the perfect lip gloss – always needing to be looked at, to have an Instagram tick of approval, to have envy. Maggie wasn't sure envy was something to aspire to, and she wasn't sure it would make you happy if you had it. She thought about Alice's parents – thrice divorced, each of them, far too busy in their international rich-people dramas to spend much time on their three daughters – and once again felt a wave of pity for the beautiful, sharp-tongued girl that would have utterly horrified Alice had she known about it.

And there was little mixed-up Fliss, glancing around, checking where everyone else was; if they had finished, if she was doing it right. Her hair had grown back, almost, but she was still a little too thin. Maggie wished she could find her own way, her own method of doing the things she wanted to do. Maybe one day. Maybe Alice was right, and she did just need to be kissed.

Ismé turned in her paper first. Maggie picked it up and sighed. She had composed a protest essay about decolonising the curriculum. But it was beautifully written and clearly argued. Miss Starling was still refusing to budge, and Ismé couldn't do this in the real exam; it was far too late to change for this year. This was a problem Maggie could absolutely do without.

Finally, by noon on the second Friday, the exams were over and the girls spilled out, yelling and shouting, to the grounds, where a pale sun was gleaming weakly. PE had been suspended while they sat their exams so they were full of bursting energy that needed to be released, and the teachers turned a benign blind eye to their screeching and bouncing as they tore about, announcing how dreadfully they'd done and how little they'd studied and how they were bound to fail, in a variety of registers of convincing. In Maggie's opinion, the ones who had genuinely done badly didn't mention it at all; retreated, in fact, as soon as they possibly could.

'How are you feeling, Simone?' she said, passing through on her way to her rooms. Marking was going to start straight away, so it would be a busy week for all the teachers. Simone blushed in her usual way and shrugged, which Maggie had long learned to read meant, 'Terrifically well.'

'That's great!' she said. 'I'm so pleased!'

Simone dropped her head again. She liked Maggie, but she wished she wouldn't make such a big deal of trying to 'perk her up'.

'Not long till the Outward Bound!' said Maggie, gleefully.

The post-mocks Outward Bound outing had two purposes; one as a release valve for the fourth years approaching their GCSEs, and two to get them out of the school and allow the sixth years to sit their A-level mocks in peace. Every year had a programme devised for it to keep them quiet, more or less.

It was also, famously for the fourth years, a good chance for the boys' school and the girls' school to mix. There were various warnings in place, of course, but nonetheless, shenanigans to a certain level were accepted and, to a point, tolerated. Snogging on the bus was OK. Vanishing in the middle of the night was not, and being found in the hut of someone of the opposite sex was completely verboten. Fortunately they had used the same company for years without incident.

Technically there was kayaking, camping and self-sufficiency. In reality it was the chance to run wild, and the stricter teachers – Miss Starling, for example – were generally discouraged from going.

As had Maggie been; as a newbie she hadn't been invited, which hadn't bothered her in the slightest, as she'd thought it was camping, and camping was very much what she wasn't in the mood for. Claire enlightened her eventually though; the children were taken care of more or less by the centre staff (it was, of course, a top-level institution, with the fees to match), and teachers had some time to themselves plus three days away, and it wasn't camping, it was lodges.

Maggie still wasn't thinking much of it, until she complained about it to David, who immediately figured it was exactly what his kids needed too. He had had a rather different time of it with mock examinations, namely a lot of no-shows, a lot of people simply taking it as leave, wasted papers and tardiness despite his best efforts. Calvin had failed outright.

He should not have been quite so down: there was a notable minority, particularly in English, Mr Frise had noted, who turned up and did their best. It didn't seem much to David, but was up on last year and apparently massively up on the years previously. The school in general was used to 8 per cent or fewer of its pupils getting three A levels. Eight per cent, in a school of two thousand.

It was simply impossible, even by the law of averages, for there not to be a greater proportion of talented people in a school. It weighed David down. So much potential wasted; so many bright talents snuffed out through low expectations, lack of prospects, a simple ignorance of everything out there. He was thinking about these things, and the looming exams, while Maggie was complaining about having to buy new waterproof boots.

'We have to bring them,' he said, and in an instant, looking at his serious expression, Maggie realised he hadn't been listening to her at all, but instead thinking about his precious pupils.

She made a face.

'Where will we find *them* waterproof boots?' she said.

'We'll manage,' said David. 'Those are details. I want to bring them. Downey House can pay the fees. Tell Dr Deveral this will be it, last bit of outreach for the year. But I can't help feeling it's doing them all some good.'

'Can we pay?' said Maggie.

'Of course you can,' said David. 'Alumni money, donor money, it has gold spilling out its ears. Come on, Maggie, you know it. It shouldn't all go on making the concert sound system even better, or resurfacing the squash courts.'

'I know!' said Maggie fiercely. 'When did you turn into such a socialist?'

'I'm not remotely a socialist,' said David. 'Can't I be a little-by-little making-things-slightly-fairer-if-you-can-step-by-step-ist? Rather than heads on poles and all that?'

'I should think so,' said Maggie. 'Thank *God* Dr Deveral is in such a jolly mood these days.'

She leaned over.

'Can we share a cabin? Is it really beautiful there?'

'It is and we can't,' said David, smiling.

'I know,' said Maggie. 'But think of it! Woods! Lakes! Trees! Fresh air! Walks! Picnics! You and me!'

'And a hundred scroty teenagers,' said David. 'Whose every move we have to police.'

Maggie smiled.

'No. It'll be awesome.'

Maggie entered Dr Deveral's warm, immaculate office the following morning. Its panelled walls smelled of beeswax, the bookshelves were full, and littered with interesting objects from around the world, there were some good paintings on the walls and an absolutely staggering view out across the grass, down to the cliffs and the crashing sea beyond.

It was a lovely room; unfortunately Maggie had been plain terrified every single time she'd ever had to come and sit in it, as had most of the other people who'd entered its portals.

'Miss Adair,' said Dr Deveral. As usual, she was looking slender and well-preserved, with excellent posture. Maggie had absolutely no idea how old she was.

'Mr McDonald suggested . . . '

Dr Deveral's lips twitched.

'You can call him David,' she said. 'Also I believe he no longer works here, so that's barely relevant.'

'Oh, yeah,' said Maggie, flushing. Even though she was thirty-four years old, being in Dr Deveral's office would bring – and was strictly designed to bring – the fourteen-year-old out in anyone.

'Well, he was thinking . . . about the Outward Bound.'

Dr Deveral sniffed and cottoned on immediately.

'He wants to bring his waifs.'

'He said he called and they have spaces.'

'Do they indeed,' said Veronica, folding up her glasses. 'And who does he suggest ought to pay for this generous outing? Presumably not Phillip Dean.'

'They can't afford jotters,' said Maggie, truthfully. 'David feeds half the children breakfast in the morning.'

Dr Deveral looked at her.

'Is that true?'

Maggie nodded. David bringing in bread and muffins as well as a large flask of coffee had originally been a ploy to get an early-morning study group going. He'd been as horrified as anyone else when it became obvious how many children simply weren't given breakfast.

Dr Deveral closed her eyes. Not here, in green, gentle England, in one of the most beautiful corners of the world? She had grown up poor, in the dockside community of

Sheffield (although her accent nowadays bore no trace of it), where there were too many children to a room in many houses; children in her recollection who went without shoes. But she couldn't recall anyone going without a hunk of bread in the morning.

'I'd have to check with our board of governors,' she said. Maggie was cheered. The board of governors included Majabeen Gupta, the local GP, for whom the state of the local children wouldn't, presumably, come as too much of a surprise, and Digory Gill, a crusty squire who had the softest heart beneath it all.

'Could you?' she said.

Dr Deveral smiled.

'Out to save the world, you two, are you?' Maggie smiled back.

'It's just a bit of camping.'

Miss Starling, predictably, was firmly against.

'Well, how many girls does she want to come back pregnant?' she demanded, crossly, forgetting, of course, precisely how Dr Deveral would take such a careless remark.

'I suppose it's the kind of people you're used to,' she said to Maggie as Maggie sat innocently finishing her boiled eggs at breakfast time.

Maggie gave her a look. 'Normal people?'

Miss Starling sniffed.

'Nothing normal at Phillip Dean. Nothing normal about someone not wanting the best school for their children. Real parents will do anything to get their kids away from that place. Stands to reason the only people left don't care. Why we have to pour our precious resources into them is a mystery to me. And when our entire school suddenly gets addicted to drugs or starts wearing their skirts as pelmets, maybe someone will listen to me for once instead of political correctness gone mad.'

Maggie watched her leave, astounded, even as she could tell that some of the other teachers were clearly agreeing with her, and quietly nodding at one another. She bit her lip and decided to ignore it. She knew part of the ethos of Downey House was that it was old-fashioned. On the other hand, there was old-fashioned and there was the way the world actually worked. She thought back to them all discussing *Great Expectations* that day. No. It was absolutely worth it. It totally was.

'I wouldn't want to be a slag,' Fliss was explaining to Simone.

Fliss was kind of talking to Simone but really it was the kind of talking where you're trying to justify yourself to yourself out loud for something you really want to do. It wasn't a conversation, as such, she just needed Simone to keep nodding. Simone's interest in matters of the heart was confined to her own romance, and faint concern that being separated from Ash was giving him a very unrealistic picture of their lives when he turned sixteen, and what she was actually like. She felt like she was becoming Estella, which was not what she had in mind at all.

'I just ... I just want to ...'

'Get shagged,' added Alice helpfully.

'It's the patriarchy, man,' observed Ismé from her bed. 'Fuck 'em.'

'All of them?' said Fliss, seriously. 'Actually, I was only thinking about one of them.'

She sighed and pulled up a picture of Calvin she'd found on the 'gram of one of the girls at Phillip Dean. She was following as herself this time, very careful to put positive comments on all of Alice's pictures to divert suspicion. Alice barely glanced at them and wondered vaguely why Fliss was so keen on Instagram and so frosty in real life but didn't give it too much thought.

She showed it around.

'I'm going to see him play tomorrow. Isn't he beautiful?'

Ismé sat up on her elbows.

'When were you sixteen?'

'January.'

'So you're sixteen and a bit . . . and you want to give it up?'

'See!' said Fliss. 'Now you're talking like that. "Give it up". Like I'm a possession. Like virginity is something women have to keep. How is that beating the patriarchy?'

'Because they want to dress you as sexy and see you as meat and hand yourself over,' said Ismé blithely. 'Don't give in to it!'

'But what if I want to?' said Fliss. 'Isn't that my choice and my body and not what a sexist society says I can and can't do?'

Ismé looked at her through hooded lids.

'That's what you want to do? Fuck some rando in a forest five minutes after your sixteenth birthday?'

Fliss's voice started to wobble.

'Nooooo,' she said. 'I just . . . I mean. I just want to meet someone.'

Ismé blew out her lips.

'OK, man. Whatever. You do you. Just be safe.'

Fliss was fuming. She thought announcing she was thinking about having sex would be quite a cool idea, but here they were, disapproving again. Simone was simply staring at her in open-mouthed horror.

'Well, I'm not saying . . . I'm just saying I could.'

'Yeah, legally you can, in a law set by some bloke who wants to fuck you,' drawled Ismé. 'But if you're ready, man . . .'

121

'Ash and I are going to wait,' said Simone immediately.

'For what, his testes to drop?' said Alice, and then, 'Oh my God, everyone is *so* sensitive these days,' at Simone's face.

'For marriage, actually,' said Simone, proudly. She didn't mention Ash's idea, that they get married five minutes after their birthdays.

'What about you?' said Fliss.

'They wish,' said Alice with a toss of her hair.

'Are you going to wait till you fall in love?' asked Fliss timidly.

Alice snorted.

'No! I'm going to wait till I meet someone ... worthy.'

She glanced briefly at the cover of her *Bridgerton* TV tie-in.

'Do you mean rich?'

'No! I mean ... Oh, I'll know it when I see it.'

'Will it have a yacht?'

Alice rolled her eyes. 'Only nerds own yachts,' she explained. 'Sensible people rent them. Even more sensible people get invited on by the nerds.'

'I'll write that down,' said Ismé, smirking.

'Wise,' said Alice.

And Fliss's latest bold plan took a back seat, to packing and arguing about whether they should take shoes that weren't wellingtons or not. And Ismé's Insta, which was mostly capital letter quotes, took something of a drubbing from Seo-Joon too that night.

Chapter Twenty-four

Calvin slouched into his classroom only ten minutes after their allotted time, which surprised David. He didn't think the lad would make it at all. But as he sidled in, all knees and elbows, his shy face broke into a smile.

'So?' he said.

'So!' said David. 'Now. As you know, I know absolutely nothing about sport.'

David's first and last attempt at refereeing had not gone well. There was no PE teacher left at the school after Mr Beehan had finally and officially snapped and attempted to bounce the one remaining ball off Archie Silver's head, and the staff were trying to share it out among themselves, with fairly dreadful results.

'Uh-huh,' said Calvin, who remembered it well.

'But I've been speaking to my colleagues at Downey.'

The boy tried to pretend he wasn't interested, but David could see his stance straighten up, just a little.

'According to them, you're very good.'

'What would they know about football though?'

'Not much,' agreed David. 'It's a rugby school.'

'That's a stupid game.'

'They're all stupid games,' said David. 'Let's not get into that right now. They think you've got something.' Calvin blinked. This was what David had alluded to the first time Calvin had come to choir. He had thought it might be an empty promise. He didn't know David very well. Nicholas Craig had been at the back, quiet, at the last few matches Calvin had played, watching him like a hawk.

'You know, four of their players from the last few years have gone on to play for the national team. Four! That's amazing.' Calvin shrugged.

'What sport is it?'

'And two of them went to the Olympics. The Olympics, Calvin. You know, if you did well, the world would be your oyster.'

Calvin had moved forward into the room, looking intently at David.

'What sport?'

David put his hands on the desk.

'Hockey.'

'HOCKEY?' Calvin looked ready to laugh. 'Ice hockey?'

'Normal hockey. You're fast and you have ball control.'

'That's a girls' game!'

'Nope,' said David. 'In fact, male hockey is a growing sport.'

Calvin shrugged. 'So? Sorry, Mr McDonald, I want to play football.'

'Listen,' said David, 'you know the scouts have been round.'

Calvin shot him a glance.

'They've seen you. They've seen you play. You're good, Calvin, nobody's denying that. But they haven't picked you up. You had, what, one trial for Exeter boys?'

Calvin shrugged.

'It's not enough. Whereas great facilities, amazing opportunities, the full weight of Sport UK behind you ... with something else, you could do amazing things. Get chances other kids don't get.'

'To play a girls' game at some bender's school?' said Calvin dismissively. 'No thanks, mate.'

Fortunately, he was not a man who took no for an answer.

David felt heartbroken when he saw the crowd at the game. Everywhere there was family, dressed up, excited, shouting already either for or to their offspring. It was a bright spring day. Maggie had marking, but David had followed the boy here and joined Mr Craig.

He didn't want to stand out but if he'd known he'd be the only person here for Calvin, he would have felt even more strange, listening to people talk the odd lingo of sport he didn't understand.

Everywhere there were dads and lads, repeated patterns of freckles, or cow licks or long legs.

He found Calvin warming up on his own, looking awkward and nervous.

'How's it going?' he said, trying to find the right tone. Calvin just shrugged.

'OK. How's your nan?' Calvin shrugged again.

'Tired,' he said.

'OK,' said David.

Calvin looked at him again.

'You live round here or what?' David shook his head.

'No.'

Calvin gave him a look.

'I just want you to do well, that's all.'

Calvin half-smirked.

'Are you sure? Won't it ruin your hockey world-domination plans?'

David smiled ruefully. 'Yes, that would be awful.'

A stern-looking man in a suit with a loud and expensive overcoat was shouting directions at the group of nervous jiggly young lads who were bouncing up and down in front of him, trying not to betray how desperately important their shot was. Calvin looked cool, focused. Maybe, thought David. Maybe this would be enough.

As soon as the whistle blew, the boys exploded with life. They were incredibly fast, thorough, quick in their movements. David could barely follow the ball. He wasn't interested in the outcome, particularly, but he was impressed with their grace, even the squattest, uncomeliest of lads, full of pimples, with little Shrek noses, had been invited along because they had something; and leaping high, diving into the scrum of players, dancing the ball along their toes, shouting, waving, they were transformed. He smiled, and watched Calvin anxiously. The boy was prowling in defence, watching the ball like a hawk, waiting for his moment, hanging back. Come on, David said to himself. Come on. The ball shot his way and Calvin lunged for it; but too late. He missed it.

'Hello, Mr McDonald!' said a little voice suddenly. He whisked round. A short figure with roughly chopped blonde hair was looking up at him tentatively. He tried to place it and finally did so; it was one of Maggie's girls.

'Felicity Prosser?' he said, and she beamed at him. She had a huge crush on him from second year, which had never quite dissipated.

'What are you doing here?' he asked in consternation. 'It's Saturday. Don't you have games?'

Fliss shrugged. 'Didn't make the team,' she said. She didn't care an ounce; Hattie could carry the sporting honours. Through careful following of Calvin's schedule she'd managed to figure out where he was. Looking around, David realised that, dotted here and there, were both his pupils and a couple of other Downey girls, and boys, those old enough to

126

leave on the weekends. They were genuinely come together. He was unbelievably delighted.

'Really?' he said, smiling suddenly. 'Does Calvin know you're here?'

He looked at the lanky boy, all alone on the defensive section of the pitch, furious with himself for missing an obvious kick. The stern-looking men in suits weren't paying him any attention at all, instead focusing on a squat little striker who looked like a pug dog but appeared to be moving like a flash of lightning.

David looked around. There were more and more faces in the crowd he recognised. Obviously word had got out. He beckoned them over to him and, half-smiling, half-embarrassed to see a teacher out of school, they mooched over to him, in dribs and drabs, ones and twos. David rallied them together and pointed them in Calvin's direction.

'CALVIIINNN,' the girls screamed, waving.

The expression on Calvin's face when he saw them all was comical; a mixture of embarrassment and happiness. The boys and girls, too, started greeting each other. It was a freezing morning and there was lots of jumping up and down and batting of hands together. David went to the little cabin and bought everyone a hot chocolate. There was some good-natured ribbing as to whether he thought they were too young for coffee but they were all pleased, and every time Calvin made a move towards the ball or started forwards, they all screamed his name with gusto, David included. The scouts turned round; clocked the boy with the fan club. That kind of thing mattered too.

It all happened in the last seconds. The ball had rebounded from the crossbar and was heading back up the pitch again. Calvin was right in its way, and he threw himself towards it, his body stretching out in the cold winter sunlight; suddenly, impossibly, he found a space through the horde of boys – a clear shot, just over the centre line.

For once, David could almost see it; almost get the reason people instilled sport with quasi-religious qualities; it felt like time slowed down. The entire park held its breath as the sun hit the frost and the lanky lad pulled his foot back all the way as if he had all the time in the world; as if it were not him but physics that compelled what was unfolding on the stage. The leg propelled forwards like a bullet from a gun and hit the ball with startling force and velocity. There were sharp intakes of breath all around as the black and white globe shone and spun in the air, fired forward, its curving trajectory towards the goal; even the keeper staring at it in disbelief, as if powerless in front of it. Then BANG, it clipped the edge of the post and bounced back into play just as the whistle blew for the end of the session, drowning out the groans of dismay echoing round the park.

David was so glad they were all there to comfort him, pat him on the back. It would have been worse if he'd been alone. He glanced around for the scouts, but they were buzzing round the short lad who'd whacked in two goals as if he was out taking a stroll. His bullet-headed dad was standing, utterly puffed up with pride. The girls were doing their best to make Calvin feel better, telling him it wasn't over. But it was, and he knew it. He changed mournfully and brushed aside David's offer of hot chocolate.

'So,' said David pragmatically. He couldn't offer the lad a lift, but he walked him to the bus stop. 'Hockey then?'

Calvin sagged even more. 'Come on, mate. I'm shit.'

'You're great,' said David. 'That school needs you. All you have to do is pass four GCSEs.'

Mr Craig nodded. 'I'll talk to the scholarship committee,'

he said. 'But you're our partner school – that should count for something.'

Calvin laughed.

'I've got no more chance of that than I do of playing for Man City,' he said bitterly.

'Yeah, you do,' said David.

'How?' said Calvin, sniffing.

'You've got me,' said David.

Chapter Twenty-five

It was March, but cold; wet weather was still tearing in across the Atlantic in sheets. Maggie looked out and sighed. This was not at all what she'd had in mind. She'd figured there might be a bit of wandering by beautiful brooks; picnics, perhaps, while wearing a flattering hat. This, however, was rather more 'curling up in front of the fire reading a book' weather. Much more. She stared at the window, despairingly, as Claire kicked back on the sofa with French *Vogue*, laughing at her.

'You told me to go!' said Maggie. 'You said it was brilliant! Why aren't you going?'

'Because you are going for me!' said Claire. 'This is indeed excellent, *non*? I shall take a very long bath.'

The length of time Claire spent in the bathroom was the only bone of contention in an otherwise uncommonly happy flat-sharing arrangement.

'So many hours in the bath!'

'Do they have baths at the Outward Bound?' said Maggie. Claire's laugh tinkled through the pretty sitting room at the top of the school.

'Aha, *non*.' She shook her head. 'One shower room for everyone. But one for teachers.'

Maggie sniffed.

'Well, I don't care. I'll be taking midnight dips with David anyway.'

Claire looked at her.

'They are very streect.'

'Oh come on, it's the country. We'll find something.'

Claire picked up the papers lying on the table, then giggled.

'What?'

'You see who you are sharing with?'

Half a dozen teachers were going, including Janie James and Thea Offili, whom she liked very much. Maggie's assigned room partner was ...

'Oh God. No.'

Claire just laughed as June Starling's name appeared.

'Sooo *romantique*,' said Claire, looking out again at the pouring rain.

Calvin put his headphones on, pulled up his hood and sank deep into himself in the back of the bus. There was going to be banter, and chanting, and all the usual nonsense, and he just wasn't in the mood for it today. His grandmother hadn't been well and he wasn't thrilled about leaving her; he really was not looking forward to going to some stupid Outward Bound whatever camp.

His grandmother's church had done something similar when he was small and he still remembered the sting of looking around, as that bus had taken off, and realising, with absolute clarity, somewhere deep in the pits of his belly – had someone said something, had he overheard something? – that he was poor. But now, with these other kids, something was being made very plain to him. Some people got to go on holiday with their families, and some didn't, and this was where he was. He was used to living with his grandmother, he knew lots of people did, and his mum couldn't always take care of him. He knew that.

But to know, to know for sure that you were absolutely the only kids whose caregivers couldn't take them on holiday – all the forced jollity of the volunteers and the staff couldn't take the stain of that away; neither could the curious stares of other children staying at the holiday place, with their families, of course. They looked at the church children as if they were prisoners on day release. It stung.

His friends caught the look on his face, without necessarily understanding it, and happily left him alone as they threw wrappers at one another and slagged off the forthcoming trip noisily, but not so noisily that the bus driver stopped the bus and threw them all off again. David was inclined to leave them to it; it should be exciting. He thought of the Downey Boys, who were expected to sit perfectly still the entire way, possibly listening to a lecture on the flora and fauna. Well. One thing at a time.

Also, his mind was distracted. He was worrying about Maggie and, specifically, the Easter holidays. Their last two holidays had not worked out at all. He was too scared to ask her if she was going back to Scotland. And it felt ... it felt like they were slipping, somehow. Their great passion of last year was still there, but in such danger of being swamped by work, by kids and marking and ...

He bit his lip. This was his fault, he knew. He had drawn back, so shocked by her devotion to her family; unsure even now of where he stood.

He knew she was confused by it, because she didn't ask him about the future, didn't make plans. They talked about work and the schoolkids as if they were talking around what really mattered.

He felt if he didn't move forwards somehow, they would start to atrophy; that if their relationship wasn't moving, it was frozen.

But it was worse than that. Deep down he was terrified she would leave for good, that the pull of Scotland would be just too strong. He couldn't swim into deeper waters, couldn't bear to probe and, eventually, get an answer to that question, in case that answer was no.

He sighed, and glanced back at Calvin, hoping he was listening to what he had sent him.

As if reading his mind, Calvin, slumped in a very back corner, slowly opened his eyes, caught David looking at him and gave a slight smile.

'I give Pirrip as my father's family name, on the authority of his tombstone and my sister – Mrs Joe Gargery, who married the blacksmith. As I never saw my father or my mother, and never saw any likeness of either of them (for their days were long before the days of photographs), my first fancies regarding what they were like were unreasonably derived from their tombstones. The shape of the letters on my father's, gave me an odd idea that he was a square, stout, dark man, with curly black hair ...'

This was pouring into Calvin's ears, at a volume his mates couldn't hear.

Fliss was also sitting apart from the others on the bus, who were moaning their heads off about the entire enterprise and being unkind about Maggie, who was patently over-excited and wearing a pair of rolled-up jeans they had all decided were ridiculous. Teachers shouldn't try and wear normal clothes anyway. The girls treated dating a teacher – a Phillip Dean teacher as he now was – as completely incomprehensible, disgusting beyond all reason, and, convinced they were going to end up with smart, successful lawyers and bankers, or in Fliss's case a famous footballer, unbelievably trashy.

*

Simone was reading a textbook. This Outward Bound was making her terribly anxious. She was not at all sporty and had barely been to the countryside when she had first arrived at Downey House. Animals scared her, and she was worried she would be made to perform physical tasks like scrambling down a rope or getting in a canoe or something. And all the rough kids would be there. She knew Fliss liked the look of some of the rough boys and Alice thought it was bizarre, but Simone was scared.

Even Simone had a boyfriend, thought Fliss. Everyone had a boyfriend, or a girlfriend, or knew what they were doing. Everyone except her. She was the only teenager in the world who had ever been like this, and felt so alone.

She leaned her head against the window and thought about Calvin. It would be cool to have a boyfriend like that. She wondered for a moment if it would upset her parents. No, they would absolutely love him, she saw at once – it would give her mother a chance to show off about how totally cool she also was. She'd insist on introducing him to all their friends. Ugh.

She sighed.

Chapter Twenty-six

The camp was deep in the woods, just on the edge of Dartmoor. A bumpy, much-pitted track led to it, past odd-looking structures like knobbly climbing walls, a carved wooden totem pole – that's well dodgy, observed Ismé as they went past.

There were ropes slung up high above the trees, and several muddy kayaks in bright shades sat on a trailer near a large boat shed; beyond it, presumably, the lake itself.

The young instructors were lined up to greet them with large grins on their faces, and there was much noise and chaos as the girls retrieved their bags from the bus – Miss Starling had done the searches to attempt to ensure there were no high heels or inappropriate garments (on the last night there was a disco), but the bags still bulged, to Maggie's eyes, with rather more than just PE kit and tracksuits.

'Oh *God*,' said Alice, in consternation. 'They're going to tell us all to drop and give them fifty. This is *hell*.'

Ismé looked at her.

'Dramatic much?'

'Oh yes, sorry, I forgot that everyone on earth who isn't me lives in timbered shacks and would be incredibly grateful to have the chance to do fifty push-ups because they haven't got any arms,' retorted Alice.

She clambered down the steps.

'Actually,' Alice said to Fliss, 'shall we pretend it's an incredibly expensive spa where they deprive you of everything and shout at you but it's in the German foothills and we're all going to lose five kilos?'

Fliss started to smile despite herself.

'OK,' she said.

The Downey Boys' coach and the two Phillip Dean coaches were already there. There was quite a lot of trainer refusing for David's kids, who didn't want to step down in the mud. The OB place already guaranteed they had all the wellies and waterproofs they could possibly need, and it couldn't come fast enough as far as he was considered. Everyone, more or less, was in very smart tracksuits in pastel colours. One or two were in their school uniforms without ties. David had checked and knew there were several spare plain black tracksuits in the facility and reminded himself to fetch them. If it was up to him, they'd all wear them.

A young woman with short, dark hair and a no-nonsense jaw stepped forward.

'Hi, everyone! I'm Mercy. I'm your camp leader for the week. Along with Ashok, Cammy, Lou and Klay!'

The other camp hosts waved cheerfully, as if they were arriving in Butlin's. This lot wouldn't know Butlin's if it bit them on the arse, thought Maggie, remembering an incredibly fun week in Ayr when they had been a lot younger, her and Anne going on the fairground rides every single day. It had been paradise.

The two schools lined up. Maggie shot a glance at David, then saw Miss Starling with her eyes on her sharply as if expecting exactly that, and immediately stared at the mud.

'Well, I hope you're going to have a *great* time here,' said Mercy. 'We're going to give you a safety briefing.'

'Nothing fun *ever* started with a safety briefing,' murmured Alice.

'Then we're going to play some ice-breaker games and I think it might even be lasagne tonight!'

'Kill me,' said Alice.

The huts were perfectly clean and comfortable but very basic; linoleum floors, a large rec room that doubled as a dining room, then dorms on one side for girls and a separate block for the boys, provoking the usual ridiculous double entendres from the Downey boys.

After unpacking – Maggie had not been wrong, there was an astonishing amount of expensive make-up on display, which, given the sinks were in a communal bathroom, meant a bit of jostling for space. It wasn't that often that Downey Girls had the chance to hang out with the boys, and they were planning on making the most of it.

Tracksuits were discarded in exchange for jeans – no need to look slutty, or attract the ire of Miss Starling – with crop tops, which were so ubiquitous as to be unremarked upon, but showed off neat little tanned tummies. Simone looked at them and sighed, pulling on a jumper, even though the evening sun had come out and it was actually rather pretty out there, the cabins softening in the golden light, the waves lapping along the shoreline.

There were four bunkbeds per room – eight children – and the Downey girls had stayed in their four, with four girls from PD over too. Simone smiled shyly and said hello – she recognised their faces now and they seemed all right. Alice kept on scrolling on her phone, making exaggerated sighs and announcing how much everything sucked, which came as a bit of a surprise to Carey, Jenna, Happy and Patricia, who had up until this point been rather enjoying themselves and looking forward to everything.

They looked at Alice, uncertain that they were meant

to be hating it. Patricia had an undercut that looked a lot better on her than Fliss's still-not-quite-grown-out pixie cut. Carey had feathery hair and a worried expression; Jenna and Happy were both sweet, round-faced girls, obviously close friends.

'It might be cool?' said Fliss, looking out into the setting sun. She wished her dog was there. 'I think there's horses and stuff.'

Alice sniffed theatrically.

'They won't be *horses*. They'll be poor old nags, carrying around sacks of potatoes. What do you reckon, Ismé?'

Ismé shrugged.

'I'm an urban cat, innit?'

The four Phillip Dean girls looked even more startled.

'I was quite looking forward to the kayaking,' said Happy, who was soft and seemed keen. Simone envied how her close-knit group of friends looked neither glamorous nor fancy, but down to earth and accepting. 'Apparently, the second last night we all paddle out to an island and there's a bonfire and we camp out under the stars? And there's a sausage sizzle.'

'Oh *God*,' said Alice again. Simone smiled.

'That sounds all right,' she said, lying through her teeth. She thought the idea was awful. 'Although I'd probably capsize a kayak.'

'Me too!' said Happy. 'That's my only fear.'

'Don't be stupid,' said her friend, Jenna. 'You're not big at all. You're gorgeous.'

'No, *you're* gorgeous,' said Happy instantly and they smiled at each other.

'Neither are you,' said Jenna, looking at Simone. 'You just have amazing knockers. The boys will capsize first anyway, they'll all be idiots.'

'And they'll be looking at my knockers,' said Simone, in such a droll voice everybody laughed, even Alice.

'I wouldn't mind capsizing if Mr McDonald rescued me,' offered Carey. The others squealed heartily.

'He's your teacher?' said Fliss, unable to keep the tone of jealousy out of her voice. She'd never really thought of him teaching girls before. She wondered if he read out love poetry to the class.

'Oh yeah,' said the girls. 'He's a *really* good teacher.'

'I knew he would be,' said Fliss grumpily.

'He dates our English teacher,' said Simone.

'No way, really?' said Jenna. 'We couldn't find him on social media or anything. It's like *so weird.*'

'I thought he might be gay,' said Carey.

'Oh my God,' said Alice, putting a pillow on her head. 'Deliver me from the children.'

Mercy took them into the kit room and they experimented with the unflattering red and yellow waterproofs, laughing and taking endless photos of each other before the phones were removed until the last night. There was no signal down in the valley anyway, and Mercy reminded them they couldn't post anything on their social media (or at least, as she secretly acknowledged, anything with the camp logo on it. Otherwise, trying to stop teenagers from doing that was going against the rising tide).

Before dinner they sat in a circle, throwing bean bags at each other and playing two truths and a lie, which mostly came down to people pretending to have iguanas at home out loud while everyone secretly noted who they fancied.

Maggie and David were at opposite ends of the room. Maggie had noticed the girls sharing rooms with her form were all suddenly staring at her in a slightly bemused way, which made her feel terrible. Yes yes, I know my boyfriend is very charismatic and I look very normal, she felt like announcing to them. She didn't dare to let her gaze stray over to where he was throwing out waterproofs to the boys so quickly that they didn't have time to refuse to put them on; insisting on wellies so they could keep their trainers clean, discreetly, she knew, passing out packets of Primark socks to boys who didn't have enough clean ones to change into.

He'd brought Stephen Dedalus as well, who was cheering up everyone, and being of particular comfort to the occasional child who, even at fifteen or sixteen, wasn't entirely comfortable being away from their parents for the night. For all the bravado, some of these kids had been ... not molly-coddled exactly, David thought, but held close, especially the recent arrivals in the UK. He didn't think it was worse than being sent to boarding school at eleven. But he was glad he had brought Stephen Dedalus nonetheless. He just had to get them not to feed him any snacks.

'You have to listen to me,' Mercy was saying now. 'Once we're on the water, it's dangerous. It's not a swimming pool. We have two groups, one hiking, one kayaking, and if you feel you're in the wrong group, and you might have ... overstated your swimming ability on the form, let me know after the briefing. But it looks like we're in for some fine weather and we ought to have a great time. So – take off your waterproofs, and go enjoy your dinner. After that, the rec room will be at your disposal.'

The rec room turned out to be a few beanbags, two table tennis tables – which the Downey boys immediately took over, with ferocious competitive instincts – and, outside in the soft light, a basketball hoop. The rest of the boys immediately went and joined the court, the girls rolling their eyes or sitting in groups as the boys showed off for them, shouting, jumping and generally messing about.

'Look at them,' said Miss Starling disapprovingly. 'Those girls are half dressed.'

'They're all in jeans and wellies!' said Maggie. 'I think it's lovely – they're just being young. Letting off some steam.'

She smiled. It had, despite the wet weekend, turned into a beautiful evening. Dartmoor was absolutely gorgeous; she'd never been there before. Even driving among the ravishing little thatched-cottage villages of Devon had been an eye-opener. It was so beautiful. See? she found herself arguing with her family in her head. If you were to come to England, you'd see it isn't so bad.

If she could have, she'd have slipped off, taken David by the hand, walked into the woods. He could have told her what all the plants and flowers were. She could have pretended to listen. Perhaps she would have magically secreted two mini bottles of Prosecco (ALL ALCOHOL STRICTLY FORBIDDEN ON SITE read large signs over the hut doors) and they could have found a glade filled with bluebells and—

'So, I hear you're thinking of redoing the summer reading lists?' Miss Starling was saying, intruding on her train of thought. Maggie tried not to sound impatient as she turned round.

'Yes, I thought we should just give them a bit more to chew on?'

'But they'll be A-level students next year,' said Miss Starling. 'They'll need a thorough grounding of Hardy, Eliot, the romantic poets, the metaphysical poets . . . '

'We'll do all that too,' said Maggie, not mentioning that she hated the romantic poets, despite David's best efforts to the contrary. 'I just thought it might be time to bring in a more varied curriculum.'

'Well, I know you're not from here,' said Miss Starling tightly, 'but I think you'll find this curriculum has served England perfectly well for hundreds of years.'

Maggie kept looking out of the window. Some of the girls had joined the basketball team now, fighting for the ball, and the laughter and shouting was reaching a pitch. The children playing were all colours, all backgrounds, all with the same hopes and desires for a good life; for adventure, for excitement, for a world to open up to them. And it should be a world that opened up to all of them. Ismé was in the middle of the group, taking charge, giving the boys a telling-off for fouling. Maggie smiled to see her.

'Well,' she said, quite firmly to Miss Starling. 'Things change.'

Chapter Twenty-seven

The rooms for teachers had only two beds, rather than eight, and their own bathroom, but even so, it was incredibly awkward getting into her pyjamas in front of Miss Starling.

Maggie wished Claire could have come, but she was out of luck. Next door, Thea Offili and Janie James were giggling away and having a grand old time by the sound of things, she thought. They would be delighted if she showed up (Mrs Offili had in fact brought a bottle of rum and would dare them to chuck her out), but then she'd have to leave Miss Starling, who certainly wouldn't want to come, and it was hardly a good look. She was still her boss.

So instead she got undressed in the bathroom and they sat up stiffly in bed reading their books – Maggie's was Kiley Reid, Miss Starling was reading Trollope – listening to the giggles from next door, the girls settling down in the dorms and, as everything gradually fell silent, the sounds of the moor and the water at night; a lonesome bird peeping, an owl's hoot, a distant splash.

Maggie lay in her bed feeling ridiculous. David was right there. Well. A few feet away, over in the boys' buildings. She hadn't seen him properly in a week. She craved his touch, the feel of him, the smell of him. But she was completely under wraps; practically in prison.

Miss Starling sniffed loudly and turned over in her sleep. Maggie fumbled for her phone under the blankets but there was, of course – as the centre proudly advertised – no mobile signal out here on the moor. It was ridiculous, she missed him so much. She sighed, tossed and turned, eliciting more sighs from Miss Starling in their turn, which eventually became heavy regular snores – and Maggie lay there in a grump, cross with the universe, wide awake. So much for the midnight walks and romantic outings; David hadn't said a word to her all evening.

David lay by the window, sharing with Mr Craig, the PE teacher to whom he had not very much to say, but David didn't mind that. He had a book but, best of all, Maggie was nearby. He lay in the single bed, looking up through the treeline to the clear stars, which promised a fine day tomorrow. The boys and girls had all gone to bed at eleven without much fussing – in fact, he thought, one or two, who never got told when to go to bed, were rather enjoying the novelty. Three days of precious freedom and fun lay ahead for the children. Fresh air and plenty of plain food and no worrying about gangs or homes or exams or anything else. And his darling Maggie was there. Perhaps it would be all right.

Breakfast was porridge, followed by bacon and eggs and plenty of toast, and it was a clutch of happy, slightly nervous teenagers who got into their waterproofs and stood on the banks of the lake. The weather was more settled than it had been; there was a cool breeze in the air, but the sky overhead was blue with scudding clouds and it was pleasant to be outside in the spring air.

Mercy was frowning at the sign-up sheet.

'We have too many kayakers,' she said. 'We'll need to move some of you.'

There was a general groan.

'Any volunteers?' she said, but nobody moved.

'OK,' she said. 'Walkers over here.'

The cliff walkers moved to the side. Fliss immediately saw Calvin among them. And that was Mr McDonald's group too. Maggie had realised at breakfast when she saw the sign-up sheet and had tried to switch, but Mrs Offili couldn't get in a kayak because of her dodgy hip, so that was that.

Simone had been eyeing the kayaks with panic all morning. She had been joking with Patricia, Happy and Carey the night before, but now they were all here and were going to be expected to put on a wetsuit. She just couldn't. She had tried. Maybe if it had been just with the girls she already knew, or maybe just girls in general ... But, looking at the groups of laughing boys – some of the them were well over six foot tall, they weren't boys at all, they were men. She was absolutely terrified of everyone who wasn't Ash and she couldn't even text him.

She knew – Miss Adair was always saying – that she should try and do things that scared her, that she should push herself out of her comfort zone, try out all the amazing things the school had to offer her, like kayaking, for example.

But she couldn't. She just couldn't.

As soon as Mercy started separating the walkers and the kayakers, she threw up her hand. 'ME!'

Fliss was standing right behind her, weighing up the Calvin situation, and was just a touch too late.

'OK,' said Mercy, nodding at Simone. 'Off you go. And you two ...'

She indicated another group, where the deep desire not to venture into cold water had overcome the natural tendency not to draw attention to yourself in a public situation.

David was wearing a large waterproof overcoat and a flat

cap which did not suit him in the slightest, and the Downey House and Phillip Dean boys joined together in slagging him off mightily for it as they set off for the cliff path, Stephen Dedalus trotting behind cheerfully, happily accepting pats from all and sundry.

Maggie watched him go – he hadn't said goodbye, but he couldn't, could he? Not in front of everyone. There was nothing to be done about that.

Then she sighed, not remotely looking forward to her job for the day – standing on the shore, helping students coming in from kayaking, making sure everyone was fine, dealing with minor scuffles, packed lunch mix-ups and anything else that came up. She didn't see why Mrs Offili couldn't have done it.

She had a radio in her mackintosh pocket and, even though the day was sunny, the wind was chill enough if you were standing still. It was odd, too, to be without her phone outside the classroom. She'd forgotten how useful it was just to have something to fiddle with when you were a bit bored. Miss Starling had somehow procured a folding deckchair – how on earth had she managed that? thought Maggie – and was sitting on it wrapped up in several jumpers doing marking.

Meanwhile, the shouts and screams of the children taking to the water passed back, the droplets turning to diamonds in the sunlight, as they collided, got wet, splashed one another, and generally had the time of their lives, carefully watched by the centre staff. Observing them, Maggie couldn't help it. She felt old.

'Now *this*,' David was saying, 'is lichen, always best growing in chalk ...' His voice meandered on as the raggedy group headed up the cliff, some of the less fit members huffing and heaving already. David slowed down to wait for them, respect-fully, calling back the others who were going ahead. It was not fair that the richer kids were healthier. Not in the slightest.

Calvin, loping ahead up the cliff side, turned round quickly, and one of his ear buds popped out and fell down. Simone, who had been at the front of the stragglers, trying to look as if she was absolutely fine – there was so much com-pulsory sport at Downey Girls you couldn't be completely out of condition, it just wasn't possible, but even so – found herself right in front of them and bent down and picked up the tiny plastic bud.

As she was about to hand it over, she heard what was coming from it. Calvin's face was comically dismayed as he swiped it back from her open hand. They looked at each other.

'Was that—'

'Ssh, man,' he said.

'But ... is that *Great Expectations*?' said Simone, so sur-prised she found herself speaking to a strange boy, which was further out of her comfort zone than kayaking.

He shrugged.

'It's the set book, innit.'

He glanced around but there was nobody else close by.

'I know, I just thought ... are you just reading it again? Is this just extra revision?'

He shook his head.

'No. I can't make head or tail of it.'

'Oh but it's *great*,' said Simone, despite herself. Calvin looked at her.

'Seerz?'

Simone nodded. 'Is Mr McDonald not teaching it to you?'

'Yeah, all year, but I wasn't really paying attention. Then, there's this thing ... well. Whatever. I want to pass my exam.

And he wanted me to read it first. And my reading ... isn't brilliant. So. He sent me a talking book version.'

Calvin stared at the ground, as if embarrassed.

'Oh, which one is it? Is it the Matt Lucas?'

He frowned.

'What do you mean?'

'Well, who's reading it? The Matt Lucas is funny, but I like the Harry Lloyd. He just has such a beautiful voice. You just believe it.'

'Huh,' said Calvin, astonished that someone would actually do this. 'So it changes depending on who is reading it?'

'Of course. Everything does.'

They fell into step – Simone only slightly puffing to keep up – as they marched up to the top of the cliff. Down behind them, sparkling on the lake, the bright red and yellow kayaks looked like spilt Lego on the floor.

Simone explained the basic outlines of the story, and Calvin started to laugh.

'Why is it funny?'

'Oh, man. It's what Mr McDonald is trying to do to me.'

'What do you mean?'

'He wants me to get a scholarship to your posh school. Play hockey or some stupid bs sport.'

Simone looked at him.

'Seriously?'

'I know,' he said. 'Which means I have to pass these stupid GCSEs. Which, who cares, man, you know?'

Simone smiled.

'Well ... I'm a scholarship kid.'

He looked at her for the first time, taking her in.

'Yeah?'

'Absolutely. My dad runs a takeaway in London.' She shrugged.

'Wow,' said Calvin. 'I'm not being funny, but what sport do you play?'

She burst out laughing. 'It's an academic scholarship, not a sporting one.'

'Oh.' He nodded. 'I didn't know they did those.'

They walked on.

'So,' he said, 'is it worth it? Do you like it?'

Simone shrugged.

'I . . .'

She thought about it.

'It's a bit weird,' she confessed, finally. It was odd. Calvin looked so scary and cool and tall but was actually easy to talk to.

'They're all so . . . I mean. They're so rich, and they don't even realise it. Fliss thinks she's poor because they stay in hotels when they go on holiday four times a year, rather than stay in their houses in other countries. And she has a *horse*.'

Calvin laughed.

'And they just . . . they just don't care about anything. They buy stuff online they don't even want, and don't send it back or anything. They just get *stuff*.'

'What's the point of going to school then? If they've already got everything? Why do they even care?'

'Because . . . because it's good to learn stuff?' said Simone, aware she sounded like the world's biggest dweeb.

'Sounds awful,' said Calvin.

Simone looked out to sea.

'It isn't,' she said. 'The teachers . . . they really care. Everyone cares all the time whether you want them to or not. They care that you're taking exercise, that you're sleeping enough, that you eat right and that you're doing your best. When I got past the maths A-level syllabus, they brought a tutor in, just for me, once a week, who'd been to Cambridge. Cambridge!'

'I don't know what that is,' said Calvin. 'But it sounds good.'

'It's amazing,' said Simone. 'It's just ... well, you like Mr McDonald, right?'

He nodded. 'Well, I think so. He's a bit weird. And it seems a bit weird he's taking so much interest ...'

Simone shook her head.

'Well, it shouldn't. At Downey, they're all like that. All over you, trying to get the very best out of you. However they can. In fact, they don't even believe you when you say you've done your best. They always think you can do better.'

'Oh,' said Calvin.

Simone looked at him. 'What do you want to do?'

Calvin shrugged. 'I wanted to play football. But apparently I can't.'

'Well, in that case,' said Simone, 'why not try the stupid books?'

He smiled at that, and then, wiping it on a tissue, he offered her one of his ear buds.

'Want to listen with me and explain what's happening as we go along?' he said.

'OK,' said Simone. 'But I'm telling you now, the Harry Lloyd is better.'

Fliss had not enjoyed a morning of learning how to capsize in a kayak and swim out from under it. She could do it well enough – her parents had a pool at home – it was what it did to her hair that was the issue. It was now plastered against her head, and her make-up was non-existent, making her look like a twelve-year-old girl again. Ismé, meanwhile, had her hair in tight plaits that shimmered in the sunlight, the drops of water on her skin making her look more beautiful than ever. Alice managed to look lithe and elegant in a wetsuit, which was frankly totally unfair. So Fliss could not believe it when, to cap it all, Simone sashayed up at the meeting point not only walking next to Calvin, but wearing one of his ear buds, which basically meant they were engaged. She was furious.

Packed lunches were opened, and moaned over, as was traditional, but in the little cove at the bottom of the cliff, a pebbly lakeside beach, with a couple of windsurfers visible on the horizon, and the sun shining down, it was hard to be entirely upset.

Maggie got a lift in a Land Rover coming round the long way on the road and was a bit behind when she and Miss Starling got there, carrying extra water refills and a box of home-made biscuits the kitchen had rustled up. By the time she arrived, everyone was already in their groups, talking about the events of the morning, and she found herself feeling oddly shy. David was surrounded by a group of lads, as ever, nerds and the awkward squad who gravitated towards him. Would she always have to share him, she wondered, with boys and girls who needed him?

In the water, a couple of the girls had rolled down their wetsuits to enjoy the feeling of the sun on their bodies. The boys were splashing them. Maggie kept an eye on them, but it seemed innocent enough. She joined Thea Offili and Janie, and beckoned Miss Starling over to join them. Somehow the foldable chair had reappeared.

'Does she take that everywhere?' said Janie. 'Where does she keep it? Up her—'

'Janie!' said Maggie, slightly shocked.

'Oh, come on,' said Thea. 'We're on holiday.'

'That doesn't mean we can tell *very rude jokes* about older faculty.'

'You can't,' said Thea shortly. 'I can. That woman fought my appointment and my promotion every step of the way.

She's an old bigot and I can't wait for her to retire. Which should have been about nine years ago. So she can take her deckchair and shove it up her—'

'Want some more tea?' said Janie suddenly. They had been joined by two other female teachers from Phillip Dean, both of whom were quiet and a little nervous, and one of whom, Liz, kept asking intrusive questions about terms and conditions and lots of chippy questions about privilege, which Maggie couldn't help but recognise in herself.

'Yes please,' said Maggie, holding out her mug.

Janie glanced over at David, who appeared to be acting out something from *The Tempest*. 'Seriously, Maggie, are you still hiding away from your boyfriend?'

Maggie shrugged, going pink.

'After everything you've been through, I don't think anyone would mind.'

'What have you been through?' said Liz. 'God, David never mentions his private life at all,' she sighed, rather regretfully. There wasn't a lot of eye candy at Phillip Dean.

'Never mind,' said Maggie quickly. Then, to Janie, 'Are you kidding? There'll be kissing noises if I get within ten metres of him. Ugh, no thanks.'

She smiled. 'Well, now everyone is just going to think you broke up.'

'It's going fine, thank you very much.'

'Apart from all the ignoring.'

Maggie smiled awkwardly. 'It's going *fine*.'

'I never saw you with some fey Englishman,' said Thea. 'I thought you'd end up with some Scottish bruiser. Like that lad you used to see.'

'I know,' said Maggie. 'Me too. It was, ugh, horrible when we broke up.'

'What's he doing now?'

'He was ill but he's getting better – sees more of my family than I do. We'd been dating since I was at school.'

She looked at the kids playing in the water.

'Same age as that lot. We were engaged and everything.'

'Can you imagine?' said Thea. 'They're so young. But they don't even know it.'

'They haven't the faintest idea.'

The women clinked their mugs of tea together.

'To getting older and wiser,' said Thea.

Then she glanced at Miss Starling again. 'But never *that* old.'

Suddenly there was a scream from the water. The teachers jumped up, as did the other kids in their varied groups across the sand, some shouting 'Shark', some diving for their phones in case something was happening, before remembering they were all back in their lockers.

Standing halfway out, hands desperately clutching at her bosoms while her bikini top floated out to sea, was Kelisa.

The boys immediately erupted in laughter and shouting, until a sharp yelp from David brought it down. One of the other girls dived in and grabbed the bra, the boys who were out there unable to help. It felt like everybody froze, that no one knew quite what to do.

Without thinking about it, fully clothed, Maggie grabbed a towel and waded out into the water, putting it round the girl instantly, placing her body between her and the gawpers on the beach, soaking herself in the process.

'Everyone out of the water,' shouted Mercy, but they stayed in, yelling at one another.

Kelisa was crying as they brought her to the shallow part.

'Did someone pull it off you?' said Maggie, furiously.

'We didn't!' said Bryce Richards, one of the first rugby team at Downey Boys. 'We absolutely didn't! We were messing about with seaweed! Nobody touched her.'

Kelisa looked miserable. The bikini top was very *Love Island* and didn't really look quite stable enough to hold up a ping pong ball, never mind anything else.

'We absolutely didn't,' chorused the other boys.

It didn't help, of course, that Bryce had been rude to Kelisa at Christmas time. The Phillip Dean boys were clustering around, looking menacing and spoiling for a fight.

'Come, come with me,' said Maggie, wrapping a second towel around her and taking the girl back to Liz, who had been watching, rather flapping her hands.

'Did anyone touch you?' she whispered in the girl's ear so the boys couldn't hear. Kelisa shook her head.

'It just ... pinged.'

'Pinged off,' said her friend, nodding knowledgeably.

'Are you OK?'

'Well, my tits popped out in front of everyone!' said Kelisa.

'Again,' said the friend.

'Shut it,' said Kelisa.

'There there,' said Maggie. Kelisa's bikini top was in her hand. It was an accident waiting to happen. But the Phillip Dean boys didn't look to be taking it that way.

David marched over to Mr Craig, who was standing protectively near the Downey boys.

'We didn't do anything, sir! We didn't!' they carried on yelling as he held his hands up.

'I just need to know,' he said, 'that nobody took a photo.'

Everyone immediately shook their heads. They weren't meant to have phones there. That didn't mean that nobody had, and it didn't mean that they didn't have cameras, which were allowed.

'If I find anyone with a picture, sharing or disseminating it, I'll rusticate the lot of you.'

'You can't, sir. You don't work here any more.'

'Well Mr Craig will.'

Mr Craig didn't look like he was inclined to do anything of the sort, and simply sniffed, 'Well, if she will dress like—'

'That's enough,' said David crisply. He wouldn't normally talk to another teacher like that, but he knew Kelisa's background and it had been unusual – her mother had occasionally worked as a stripper, so the last thing she needed was being shamed for it.

'Don't let me catch you treating any of my pupils with anything less than total respect.'

They looked at him, sullenly, as he turned and stalked back across the sand.

Maggie took Kelisa back to camp in the end, Mercy having her hands full trying to get the kayakers back out on the water (or in the case of the walkers, an afternoon of geocaching), and none of the Phillip Dean teachers seeming to know quite what to do. David caught up with them at the car.

'Kelisa, are you all right?'

She nodded.

'It was horrible though, them all laughing.'

'Of course it was. I gave them a bollocking.'

Maggie internally raised an eyebrow at his new-found swearing abilities with the pupils. Kelisa shrugged.

'It's just blokes, innit? Doesn't matter if they've got money, or them fancy manners they get up at that school. They're just blokes underneath. My mum taught me that.'

'Well, my job,' said David, 'is to try and civilise the bastards.'

Indeed, behind him was a large group of Phillip Dean pupils.

'We'll get them for you, Kelisa,' said one of them. 'Don't worry about it.'

Kelisa looked touched. 'Aw, thanks, lads.'

'No! Don't!' said David. 'This isn't sixteenth-century Verona! No retaliatory feuds!'

He thought about it.

'Maybe things are getting a *bit* better.'

He looked at Maggie, who smiled at him.

'Cheers,' he said. 'I'll talk to you later.'

'I'll talk to you later?' Kelisa frowned, when the two of them were in the Land Rover. 'That doesn't sound very romantic, miss.'

'We're trying to stay professional in the workplace,' said Maggie. 'It's harder than you'd think.' She looked at the girl. 'How are you feeling?'

Kelisa shrugged.

'Do you think someone had a phone?'

'They wouldn't have been able to get it out in the water quick enough,' said Maggie reassuringly. 'And if they were on land they couldn't have seen much. I'm sure you're safe.'

Kelisa exhaled.

'Are you OK though? I know it can feel bad.'

'At least the boys yell,' said Kelisa, looking moodily out of the window at the setting sun. 'The girls will all be talking about it for days.'

'I know,' said Maggie, sympathetically. 'I know.'

Kelisa kept her eyes fixed on the landscape.

'I mean,' Maggie started, 'if you've had enough ... you don't have to stay if you don't want to.'

Kelisa turned round.

'Are you kidding?' she said, as if Maggie was unfailingly stupid. 'This is the first holiday I've ever had.'

Dinner that night was a more muted affair, even though it was a barbecue outdoors, and another loamy evening. There was a rounders tournament set up for them after they got back, though, and the two schools played one another to start with. It wasn't fair though; the sporting abilities of the Downey children rapidly overtook their Phillip Dean peers, Calvin excepted, and even Mr Craig could see it, and shuffled up the teams at half time. Plus, there was a certain amount of backtalk and competitiveness, and it was in everyone's interests to keep things calm.

Fliss sat next to Simone waiting her turn. She wasn't on the same team as Calvin, couldn't see a way to get close to him at all. She was going to have to pin it all on the sleepover, or the disco, one of the two. At least she had an in now.

'So, you and Calvin are friends, I see,' she said, trying to keep the sting out of her voice.

Simone laughed. 'Not really,' she said. 'He'll be with all his cool friends now. We were just chatting.'

'What about?'

'Who does Fliss fancy now?' said Alice, taking out an ear bud. 'Is it male? Female? Fish? Dog?'

Fliss didn't say anything, specifically because if she did, Alice would probably make a point of getting off with him.

'Oh, still Calvin. Well done! Have you offered him your flower yet?'

'Stop picking on Fliss,' said Ismé. 'It's boring.'

'Yes, it is,' said Alice. '*Everything* is boring. God.'

'Well. Meet some new people. Expand your horizons.'

'So, what, I can say hello to them when they're serving me a cup of coffee one day and it's all terribly awkward?' said Alice. 'No thanks.'

To Fliss's absolute surprise, Ismé took a moment, then burst out laughing.

'I swear to God, you're getting worse, not better.'

'I am being *true to my essential self*,' said Alice, pushing her sunglasses back on her face. 'I don't want to meet people here. I want to go to the Venice Biennale. On a boat.'

'You do you,' said Ismé.

'I shall,' said Alice, returning to the copy of *Vogue* she'd brought.

'Well?' said Fliss to Simone. Calvin was coming up to bat. Without even thinking about it, he casually swung his arm and lopped the ball over the top of the buildings, and splashed it into the lake, to massed cheering from his team and groans from the other, as he started to stroll casually round the bases.

'He's thinking of going for a scholarship for the sixth form. He wanted to know what it was like being a scholarship kid.'

Ismé snorted loudly.

'Did you tell him?'

'What?' said Alice, from her towel on the grass. 'Free meals, free bed and board, an amazing education and you're basically lying out under the stars on holiday right now and eating an ice cream. Did you tell him of the terrible terrible cross you have to bear?'

'Ha ha,' said Ismé, finishing her ice cream.

'I told him he should go for it,' said Simone. 'I offered to help him if he needed it. Mr McDonald is tutoring him, but I said I could give him some extra time.'

'Maybe you could tutor me too,' said Fliss. 'At the same time.'

'Oh, for God's sake!' said Alice. 'He's *right over there*. Just stick some tissue paper down your bra and walk past him. Get Bryce to ping your bra strap off, it's about all he's good for.'

Maggie had retired to her room. It was a lovely evening, and having to spend it alone was messing with her head.

Kelisa had a loyal band of female friends rallying around her, thankfully. And some of the tensions – possibly not all – of the afternoon were being worked out on the rounders pitch.

So. That just left her. By herself, avoiding the other teachers asking her about her relationship. Too old to be in with the kids; too young to endure a night discussing cross-stitch with Miss Starling, too dangerous, in the febrile atmosphere, to be anywhere near David. This wasn't at all what she'd been expecting. She'd been naive, she allowed. But even so. He was so obsessed with the children, with school, completely to the exclusion of her.

Mercy, the camp leader, knocked on the door.

'Hey, a letter came for you.'

'A *letter*?'

Mercy shrugged.

'Is Kelisa all right?' she asked.

'I think so,' said Maggie.

Mercy frowned. 'And it was definitely an accident? We have a zero tolerance policy . . . '

Maggie winced.

'They're entitled, the Downey boys. And they're posh. But they're not bad. They were just messing about with seaweed.'

'Kids in too-big bodies,' said Mercy.

'Aren't we all,' said Maggie, picking up the letter.

The two women glanced out of the window of the room, at the laughing, shouting, happy kids in the dimming light outside.

'Oh *God*,' said Mercy. 'I love working with kids. But they can be so daft.'

'Couldn't agree more.'

Mercy glanced at the letter.

'Nice handwriting.'

Maggie rolled her eyes. 'Yes,' she admitted, knowing full well who it was from. 'He does.'

Chapter Twenty-eight

Maggie couldn't help but grin, even through her frustration as she waited for Mercy to leave, and sat down on her narrow single bed, unfolding the piece of paper. In David's lovely hand it was – she knew it would be, he was incorrigible – a poem. Larkin, she recognised immediately.

> *The trees are coming into leaf*
> *Like something almost being said;*
> *The recent buds relax and spread,*
> *Their greenness is a kind of grief.*
> *Is it that they are born again*
> *And we grow old? No, they die too,*
> *Their yearly trick of looking new*
> *Is written down in rings of grain.*
> *Yet still the unresting castles thresh*
> *In fullgrown thickness every May.*
> *Last year is dead, they seem to say,*
> *Begin afresh, afresh, afresh.*

She smiled.

How like him to realise exactly what she was feeling. How strange it was and lonely to be here, but to be without him. This made her miss him even more. She went and sat by the window, just to see him – pitching now, he appeared to have been roped into one of the teams. Despite his oft-professed aversion to sports, he had, she knew, a soft spot for cricket, and not a bad bowling arm, as evinced now as he bowled out a Downey boy, to howls and cheers. She couldn't believe they could be so near and still so far. She had to be with him. She had to. It was like a physical illness, now. Everything she could see from far off. The lithe figure, still boyish as it moved; the black hair flopping over his forehead, the huge, face-splitting grin when he managed to bowl someone out.

She wanted him, completely and utterly, couldn't bear the look of him pulling off his jacket, unbuttoning his shirt, bringing in her a terrible longing, a deep need to touch him. His face looked flushed and she wanted to be near him, hear his breath running faster and faster . . .

God.

She didn't have writing paper with her – who on earth travelled with writing paper, except the world's most infuriating man? – but she knew what she wanted to write to him, and it wasn't about buds opening up in the spring.

Turning over the page, she tried to remember it, then couldn't and had to ask Mercy to borrow her computer and tried to pretend it was urgent, but it was something to do and she got there at last.

She was feeling disconnected from David. He seemed to be getting further and further away; more and more distant. No talk of the future, or what they would do next. She was terrified they would lose it, fall back into being colleagues, into being friends. Well. No. They weren't friends.

She found exactly the verse she was looking for; four hundred years old but as filthy as the day it was written. She had to be clear, she felt, exactly what she wanted.

Licence my roving hands, and let them go,
Before, behind, between, above, below.
O my America! My new-found-land,
My kingdom, safeliest when with one man mann'd
My Mine of precious stones, my Empirie,
How blest am I in this discovering thee!
To enter in these bonds is to be free;
Then where my hand is set, my seal shall be.

She asked Mercy to deliver it to Mr McDonald in the boys' hut. Mercy's eyes went wide. 'If the kids were doing this, I'd report you,' she said.

'I know, I know,' said Maggie. Mercy looked at her sternly, with a glint of a smile.

'Are you married?'

'It's the 2020s, Mercy.'

'I meant, to other people.'

'Oh. Oh my God. No! Why, what would you have done? Do you have zero tolerance for adultery?'

'I just like to run a good clean facility,' said Mercy.

'It's true, you know, you millennials all being puritans.'

'Yes,' said Mercy. 'We saw the mess you lot made.'

And they parted, smiling.

Chapter Twenty-nine

'OK,' said Mercy the next morning, addressing the group. Maggie looked around. Things seemed calmer today; the tightly fought rounders game, won, of course, by the team with Calvin on it, had possibly defused some of the tension.

Kelisa had her praetorian guard— which Ismé appeared to have joined, interestingly. Ismé no doubt thought she was fighting on the side of the oppressed again. Well, good for her. Alice was sitting at the back, not joining in. Maggie almost felt sympathetic. In the end, there was no point in pushing things. Alice was not going to be a kayaking joining-in person in her life, and that was that. On the other hand, little chunky Simone of all people was sitting next to Calvin, the super-cool dude of Phillip Dean, chatting away nineteen to the dozen. So, there you go.

The plan was to get into the Land Rovers and get taken to the other side of the lake. The walkers were going to abseil off a cliff – there was some nervous laughter at this – and the kayakers were going to paddle to an island, where the walkers would join them for camping out, setting up shelters and tents and making their own dinner. Marshmallows would be involved, apparently. Maggie looked round the room, thinking once again how very young they were, when you saw how their faces perked up at the mention of marshmallows.

'Also, does anyone play the guitar?' said Mercy. Astrid Ulverton frowned. 'I've brought my clarinet,' she said. The Downey girls groaned. Astrid loved her clarinet more than life.

'Well, that works too,' said Mercy. 'If anyone wanted to make some music later, they'd be very welcome. We want this to be a fun time for you, and it looks like it's going to be a lovely day out on the water, so – stay safe, you guys, and go get changed.'

David found her on her way back to her room.

He grabbed her arms, pulled her inside.

'I got your letter,' he said, his breath ragged suddenly.

'Christ,' Maggie said. 'I can't bear it. I can't bear having you here and not able to touch you.'

'I have to . . . I have to . . . '

The letter was sticking out of his pocket.

He kissed her, passionately, and in an instant Maggie's brain went white; everything she was worrying about, everything that was on her mind, the worries about the children, about her family and relationship, went immediately out of her head, as she kissed him back fiercely, immediately breathless, immediately, crazily ready. She craved him, she could not speak or think when he was there, and nothing else – the complications of their lives, the uncertain future – nothing else mattered at all.

'Oh God,' he said, as she broke off, hearing a noisy calling of 'Miss Adair!' echoing through the hall, which long experience had told her that particular tone – a combination of embarrassment and panic – almost certainly meant someone had just got their period and didn't have the kit with them.

She looked up into David's dark eyes, still panting.

'I can't bear it.'

'You're driving me crazy,' he said. 'You are *so* close and I can't touch you. I can't grab you. I can't ...'

'Tonight,' she said, leaning into him, so he groaned. 'They'll all be away,' she whispered. 'Come find me.'

'I'm meant to be there.'

'Find an excuse.'

'I'll swim back.'

'Do it. You have to. You must.'

'MISS ADAIR!'

'Wait till we've gone,' she said. She ran a hand up his white shirt, felt his chest. 'I need you,' she said.

'Christ,' he said again. His hands were trembling.

She went out into the corridor, took Balina Ferse off to the supplies cupboard, and of course by the time she came back, he had gone, off with his group. But she thought of the look in his eyes and knew she'd be able to concentrate on nothing else all day. Everything now would be torture until he came. Everything without him was worthless.

She followed the kayakers in a heavy haze, her limbs liquid and her head light as the sunny air. Her bad mood was forgotten; everything faded into the background as she thought of nothing else but counting down the hours till the evening came.

It was undeniably rather lovely to be out on the water, particularly in the safety boat, a RIB which buzzed along, bouncing on the waves at impressive speed, helmed by a member of the centre staff, a tanned young man with gleaming muscles.

God, thought Maggie. She had to get a handle on herself, she was turning into a disgusting old sex maniac. She thought again of the intensity, of the desperation of David that morning, and it filled her senses completely. She borrowed the binoculars and looked for him on the cliff tops, but there was just a line of tiny dots on the horizon at this point. He was probably looking for someone to talk about birds to. She smiled happily as the spray bounced up and she applied sun cream to her freckled face and, rather in the style of Claire, who thought the sun was vulgar, put on a massive hat, which immediately flew off again. The letter had done it, she thought. Now he would focus on her.

But watching the kids laughing and jostling in their kayaks, she felt a sudden moment of happiness that they had done it; brought the two schools together, despite everyone telling them it would be an awful idea, bound to result in fighting.

The kayaks were all roped together now, and they were playing a game which involved people having to run across as many kayaks as possible before falling – often spectacularly – into the water, to great cheers and shouts of laughter. She watched a while to see if Kelisa would do it – and she did, to generous applause.

Today seemed nothing but optimism and fun. The girls had all bonded, it seemed, if the levels of chatter were anything to go by. There was a lot of common ground in who they followed on Instagram, and in their fury at not being allowed to 'gram their trip, and they were all promising to swap follows as soon as they got their phones back. And the boys were larking about. It was amazing. It might ... might just be working.

Maggie lay back, let the sun warm her skin, closed her eyes, enjoyed the sensation of the RIB bouncing across the water.

Simone caught sight of the harness at the top of the cliffs and stared at it in consternation. Oh God. This kind of thing was exactly why she'd chosen to avoid walking. They weren't seriously suggesting they got down the side of a cliff in that. 'But

I really do have a rash,' Fliss was complaining. Mercy had her arms folded. 'I just think it makes more sense for me to join the walking party.'

'We're here to accomplish goals,' pointed out Mercy. 'Not to chop and change when things suit us.'

Fliss screwed up her face and decided to try another tack.

'But my goal is to learn to kayak *and* to do abseiling,' she said brightly. 'That's why I'm having such a brilliant time. I just want to try everything. And I'm sure there's room in the Land Rover. Please?'

She was up to something, Mercy was sure of it. On the other hand, life was hard enough at sixteen. Mercy wasn't so far away from it she didn't remember.

'All right,' she said. 'But you can't change back again.'

Fliss beamed.

'No problem,' she said. 'I don't want to get into a wetsuit again anyway.'

It had, however, not been quite as easy as she'd hoped to muscle in on the Calvin situation. First of all, their room-mates, Jenna, Patricia, Happy and Carey, were also walkers, and delighted she'd joined them. Fliss realised with a start that, to them, she was quite cool.

And everywhere she looked, there was Simone, almost a foot shorter than Calvin, but their heads bent as close as they could. Fliss broke free of the group eventually and jogged up to meet them, but although they smiled nicely enough, they were absolutely in the middle of a discussion of the themes of loyalty over money and both of them were in full agreement that while loyalty obviously was excellent, definitely a bit more money would be nice and then they segued into talking about what they would buy if they had some, and Fliss could hardly bear it.

Calvin wanted some clothes and one day a car, and his own Netflix account so he didn't have to piggyback his friends' all the time; Simone said she wanted a new MacBook then, daringly, told the truth and said if she really had loads of money she'd have a breast reduction. Calvin had laughed his gentle laugh and said he was sure her boyfriend wouldn't agree with her and Simone had flushed bright red, and all Fliss could think of was the number of times her mother had offered to take her on shopping trips when she could have bought all the trainers and clothes Calvin could possibly have desired; that she had a MacBook that actually replaced the one she'd had before which she'd carelessly left on a train, and her mother had rolled her eyes, but not been that fussed before buying her another one.

And Simone would usually have included Fliss in the conversation – given her own terror of being excluded, she normally invited everybody in – but she couldn't possibly, because there was nothing, as far as she could tell, that Fliss didn't have.

'Do people make a big deal out of it at your school?' Calvin wanted to know. They did at his. Not him, specifically; his height and general popularity meant he didn't take too much grief, but he knew some kids did, with their Tesco mobiles and scuffed trainers. It must be worse there, right?

Simone shook her head.

'It really isn't,' she said. 'People look scruffy on purpose.'

'You're kidding?'

'Nope. It's like, because absolutely everyone has tons of money, they make a point of not wearing new stuff. It's really confusing.'

'I would fit right in,' said Calvin.

'You would anyway,' said Simone. 'You're just one of those people who fits in anywhere.'

Calvin shrugged, as if trying not to agree with the obvious truth of this statement.

'But yeah, it's really weird,' went on Simone. 'My mum always turns up in, like, her wedding outfit, and my dad gets the car polished and it is *so* embarrassing. Everyone else's parents turn up in jeans and crappy old Land Rovers, or like plain white trousers but you can tell they're dead dead expensive but they're just plain? It's really confusing.'

'Wow,' said Calvin. 'That's mad, man. Imagine having all that cash and not buying good gear.'

'They are so, so weird ... Oh, sorry, Fliss, I forgot you were there.'

'I see that,' said Fliss, smiling rather tightly.

They were exhausted and thirsty by the time they reached the top of the cliff, the sun shining hot on their heads. One of the other instructors was down at the bottom, and they peered over the side nervously. There were two fixed lines heading straight down and harnesses next to them.

'No way, man,' said one of the Phillip Dean boys, and the rest were inclined to agree with him.

'OK!' said the instructor. 'We're going to fasten ourselves into the harnesses, two at a time – put your helmets on, please.'

A fair amount of groaning met this, but then they fell quiet. The walking group didn't contain exactly the largest number of the braver students. Absolutely nobody was coming forwards. Some unpleasant remarks vis à vis the harnesses circulated at the back among the boys.

Fliss thought she saw her chance. She manoeuvred next to Calvin and opened her eyes wide.

'I'm so scared,' she said, looking up at his handsome face. 'Maybe we should go together. Promise you'll hold my hand?'

He looked at her in consternation.

'Are you kidding, man?' he said. 'I'm not going down there. Christ!'

Indeed, on closer inspection he was clearly sweating and extremely nervous, which just made Fliss think, seriously? have you never been abseiling before? – she had, on a trip to the Grand Canyon. Hysteria seemed to affect the group with lots of people saying absolutely no way. It was, undoubtedly, a long way down a solid cliff. Out on the lake were the bright kayaks, approaching the island. More than a few hearts deeply wished they were still at sea level.

'Listen,' the instructor was saying, 'you need to make sure you get in the harness correctly, otherwise we might lose grip of you. Come on. Let's get you going '

This didn't do anything to calm nerves. David, who was normally the first to sense this kind of thing, was miles away. He had not, in fact, as Maggie had suspected, been rabbiting on about birds.

Instead, he had been thinking about her.

About the whole oddness of them getting together, through the awfulness of Stan's illness, and the very clear hostility he had faced from her family (and the polite lack of interest she'd found in his), and the usual stresses and full-on workload of being teachers, when he couldn't even visit her at home.

He worried, all the time, that he couldn't compete with her close-knit, argumentative, loving family, and how clearly they all wanted her back in Scotland – would that eventually take its toll? People couldn't resist their families forever, not really. And would she find everything his ex, Miranda, had found irritating about him? He knew he got overcome some-times, over-involved in what he taught, what he believed in; he knew he spent too much time with his head in books, or dealing with the students, to always be as fully in the moment of his relationship as he should do. He was flawed in many ways and could they – should they – even try to live up to the idea of each other that they had in their heads; could they make their colourful imaginations a reality?

But coming here, seeing her, had confirmed something deep down in him, as solid as rock. The sun resting on her hair, the way she had run into the water for Kelisa; bursting out laughing at the boys playing rounders. He craned his neck to see if he could see her down below. She was everything; his heart, his words, the name of every love in every book he would ever read; the heroine of every novel he ever taught; the princess, the sweetheart, the witch, the queen, the song. He had to make his move, he knew. Because for the rest of his life, every turning page would be her face. He stared out to the island from the top of the cliff, as if it were Avalon: she was Hero; Miranda, Dorothea, Emma; Guinevere, and he was completely undone.

'Sir! Sir! Nobody wants to go down the cliff, sir!'

David blinked and smiled.

'Uhm . . . ' he said. There appeared to be a pupil–instructor stand off.

'Nobody wants to go,' explained one of his younger boys.

'Oh,' he said. 'And that's a problem?'

He had no idea what to do on these kinds of things and wasn't terribly interested.

'COME ON,' Mr Craig was bellowing at them. 'Get on with it.'

'Actually, we don't find that's a terribly helpful approach,' the young instructor said to David in a low voice.

'But they should do it?' said David back, looking out at the mutinous faces.

'Uh, yeah.'

'OK.'

He sighed. Better get it over with then.

'Right, I'll take the left harness. If I can do it, and I am, as you know, a pathetic weakling who is terrified of stray footballs, then you can.'

There was laughter from both schools at this. Mr McDonald's fierce reluctance to watch any sport he couldn't read a book during was well known, even though he had manfully taken on shifts at Phillip Dean, when their PE hours were cut again to half an hour a week.

He let the supervisor buckle him in.

'Come on, you can't be out-braved by a pathetic teacher,' he said. 'Who else is going to start off?'

Suddenly, an idea gripped Simone. If she went down after everyone else, they would all see her bum coming down the cliff. That was simply too unbearable to think of. No. Nobody must watch. There was only one solution. Pink in the face, she marched forward.

'I'll do it!'

'Go, Miss Pribetich!' said David, in pleased surprise. 'I knew there was a reason Miss Adair liked you,' he said to her, more quietly, as she joined him getting her harness fitted, a statement which filled her with so much pleasure she couldn't stop beaming.

'Go, you!' said Calvin, clapping loudly. 'Go, Simone!'

This had the effect of making Simone blush even harder, especially as Jenna, Carey and Patricia took up the chant too. Was this . . . was this what it was like to be *popular*?

She was so full of this emotion, in fact, that she barely noticed as the rope began to slip off the side, and she inched her way down, holding tightly onto the clip, dropping only a few centimetres at a time, in her careful, studious way.

David, on the other hand, had let his long legs get away from him, and caused much amusement from above scrabbling in mid-air. But he made it down, both thumbs aloft, and after that, when the swot and the teacher had done it, the rest came plodding steadily forwards to take their turn, pushing forward now so they didn't look cowardly, and then laughing, shouting and thoroughly enjoying the adrenalin rush. The instructor gave David a 'see' look as they were all safely reunited at the bottom and indeed, he couldn't deny the sense of achievement he saw in the faces all around.

'You were the only person that fell off,' observed one of the Phillip Dean boys.

'It is just as well,' said David, beaming, 'that I am just your English teacher rather than part of the British Antarctic Survey.'

The children fell on lunch with an appetite – it was good, healthy fare, chicken, salad, a ham and egg pie, with rice balls and halloumi for the vegetarians, and like all food eaten outside, in the sunshine, after some strenuous exercise and a bit of a thrill, tasted unbelievably good. Simone sat, her face in the sun, and thought she had never been happier in her entire life. David, staring out to sea, fingering again and again the poem in his pocket, was thinking something similar, because coming towards them was the RIB, and the person he wanted to see most in the world was on it.

Chapter Thirty

The two groups coming back together were full of chat about what they'd been up to in their separate groups, and were split and recombined to form the working party to build the shelters. They were set to plaiting branches in the heavy forest to build a canopied area for them to eat and sit in, as well as having to put up their own eight-person tents; huge, ancient old things with characteristic heavy smells that reminded Maggie of being very small and going to St Andrews with her family, and the amazing fun that entailed; it reminded David of his father's old kitbag.

Hammering in of pegs was required, and it was amazing, really, how few children had ever even lifted a hammer. But with noise and chatter, the campsite came together in a clearing and it was undeniably fun – and a little Famous Five – to be on an island. There was the ruin of a little church there, with a small toilet block behind it, and the children boggled at how you would put a church there, before David explained how when people only had the choice of their feet, their horses or a boat, the church would have been the quickest place to get to by far.

The bonfire crackled higher as the chill spring evening came in, the flames dancing up into the pink sky. As the staff started the barbecue going, and handed out Cokes to the kids, one of the instructors pulled out a guitar, to a general groaning from the kids, until he started playing a low, sweet version of 'Old Town Road', which not even the coolest of kids could resist humming along to, closely followed by 'Dynamite'. One or two of the pupils had got closer, Maggie couldn't help noticing; Patricia was sitting next to Gar, one of the likeable Phillip Dean boys, who had his arm casually slung around her shoulders. Carter, a Downey boy she didn't know, was exchanging burning hot glances he probably thought nobody else had noticed with Archie Silver, one of David's more challenging bad boys, who had a glower like a young James Dean.

Maggie sat, cosy by the fire, surrounded by the chatter of the young, and the teachers, laughing, and officially off duty. Mrs Offili and Mr Craig were staying on the duty roster in case they had to drive, so she was allowed a glass of wine, despite the pupils' ragging, and the walls felt like they had finally come down.

David couldn't concentrate. He had to tell her. Every time he glanced at her from the other side of the fire, she caught his eye, challenging, laughing. They weren't noticeably less obvious than the teenagers, whose hormone levels were driving them absolutely crazy. Mercy, in fact, was the most level-headed of them all, despite being all of twenty-five.

'So we're going to go round and say one thing we're grateful for, being here,' Mercy said. 'Team Downey-Dean.'

There was a moment's silence.

'What?' said someone.

She consulted her clipboard.

'Team Downey-Dean. That's what you're down as on the booking list.'

'I like it,' said David. 'Team Downey-Dean.'

There were general smiles and people went round and announced what they were grateful for.

Some were funny – Alice pointed out that she could get off this godforsaken moor in under thirty-six hours and get her nails fixed; lots of people mentioned not having to study for their exams; little Angela Harris mentioned not having to play hockey, where she spent a lot of time running away from the ball.

Some were sad; when Gwen Pulteney stuttered that it was just nice not to be at home, the children fell quiet, many of them perhaps reflecting on their own families; possibly not as unpredictable as Gwen's, but nonetheless.

David spoke briefly and well on how happy he was that they had all managed to come together today, that he was deeply relieved that they now knew how to weave a shelter out of branches in an emergency and that they had learned to open a tin of beans before heating it over an open flame, and thanked the course leaders for their support, which gained a huge round of applause.

Then, to Maggie's total surprise, Bryce Richards stood up.

'I just wanted to say,' he said, his voice less bullish than it normally was, 'sorry we laughed at Kelisa. I don't want any of the girls to tar Downey Boys or to think we're ... well. Public school wankers.'

There was laughter.

'But you ARE,' shouted one.

'We are,' he said. 'But ... OK. I want you to think we're respectful public school wankers. So. I'm very sorry.'

And he sat down. Maggie raised her eyebrows at David, but he didn't look as pleased as she thought he would have.

Sure enough, as the teens went back to chatting and passing round coffee, Kelisa and her friends were suddenly sitting beside Bryce and his friends, and David sensed trouble in the air. Those had been fine words from Bryce, but then, of course they were. That kind of self-deprecating charm was something that Downey boys were imbued with from birth, and the Phillip Dean boys knew it, and the girls found it attractive. There was muttering at one end of the fire, and the lovely cohesive spirit David had felt only moments before was on the verge of splitting.

He had a brief word with Mercy, who nodded, then glanced at her watch. Ten p.m. Nothing to these kids normally, of course, but it had been a hard, physical day, it was getting cold and frankly, they were all exhausted.

'OK, you lot!' she shouted. 'Time for bed! Girls in the loo first, boys next!'

There was some grumbling, not much, but as they got up, David spotted Bryce and Kelisa exchanging longing looks, touching hands. He also spotted young Silver eyeing them up, frowning.

'Come on,' he said. 'Don't start something.'

'I don't think he really was sorry, sir,' said the lad, with unusual perspicacity. 'I think he was being charming on purpose.'

'Yeah,' said David thoughtfully. 'They learn that at school.'

'Do they?' said Silver, interested. 'How?'

'I'm not sure,' said David. 'But don't fight them, OK?'

'Just a little bit?'

'No.'

Silver sighed.

'But that's how we get the girls to like us!'

The RIB took off from the island, leaving the students with the instructors. David had decided to come and sat at the back of the boat, emboldened by a glass and a half of very indifferent wine, and the sweetness of the evening. Maggie sat down next to him and laid her head on his shoulder. Liz from Phillip Dean immediately turned round to look the other way with a loud humphing noise, but Thea Offili just smiled and said, 'Don't let the kids see.'

'*Surely* we're far enough away by now,' grumbled Maggie. 'And it's our own time. And we're not nuns, we are actually people.'

'So you're going to let Miss Starling see you?'

'Christ no,' said Maggie, laughing and admitting defeat, straightening up. 'Christ, she'd hit me with her portable deckchair.'

In fact, David felt very uncomfortable with her so close, even being able to smell her. He wasn't entirely sure he could control himself. She took it as coolness, and was surprised, after that morning.

'So, how do you think it's going?' said Thea. 'Do you think they'll be all right there? Won't go too *Hunger Games*?'

'They'll do that in the morning,' said Maggie. 'With paint-balls. As a surprise.'

'It's good for them to blow off some steam,' said Thea.

'I think so too,' said Liz quietly. 'Some of them have never been outside so much in their lives.'

'Good,' said Maggie, looking back on the island where the fire was still lighting up the sky, and laughter was sounding on the air. 'I'd love to bring my nephews here. They'd love it. Every kid should get to come here.'

The boat chugged neatly to the shoreline of the camp, just by the huts. Maggie looked at David desperately – the kids were away, so surely, now? Now they could be together? Now was the time?

But everything he felt, everything that had been through his mind that day, did not, he thought, fit well in public surroundings, in shared rooms, in their jobs, however enchanting the location. It was not right, not at all. But he couldn't look at her, otherwise he would be overcome with temptation to drag her into the woods, and they would lose their jobs all over again.

'Goodnight,' he said briskly, and set off in the direction of the boys' huts.

'Not your lucky night,' said Liz to Maggie, amid generally bawdy laughter, but Maggie found it hard to laugh off, and could barely hide her dismay as she stumbled into the dark bedroom where Miss Starling was already snoring in the single bed, wearing the white nightie she had buttoned up to her whiskery chin.

Chapter Thirty-one

The next morning was wet, which suited Maggie's mood. It felt like every time – *every time* – they got close to some kind of action, some kind of way of moving their relationship forwards, even if it was one stupid walk in the woods, he would retreat again, talk in poetry, not action. You could say many things about Stan, but he knew his own mind. He had settled on her and never given her any cause to doubt his feelings – until she'd broken his heart. Whereas David was agonising, running hot and cold, and she never knew where she stood with him. She sighed. Maybe it was his being English. Maybe – and this made her want to be sick – maybe he hadn't made up her mind about her, when she had burnt every bridge; upset her family, almost broken – not quite, but even so – ties with her homeland, the place she was born. She had given up everything for him, had placed all her eggs – possibly literally, given she wasn't getting any younger – in his basket. Was it too much for him? Did he prefer the cool, reserved Miranda? Mind you, she remembered his ex fiancée had raged at his inability to commit, to be as passionate in his life as the poets he adored on the page; to care as much for her as he did for every waif and stray who crossed his path.

She barely caught his eye at breakfast: the children weren't kayaking back, but being picked up on the RIB and driven off the site: their last day after paintball was a litter-picking and wall-building environmental expedition in the morning, with team games in the afternoon. The teachers sat in the Land Rover, and Maggie didn't even look at David. The frosty air did not go unnoticed among the other teachers, who raised their eyebrows at one another.

Getting a crowd of wet, exhausted teenagers to pick up litter from the side of a main road was not easy. Several people pointed out, not entirely incorrectly, that the course charged money for them to do this work, and Alice point-blank refused to touch anything, even when cajoled, shamed and encouraged by Mercy and the other instructors, but instead made a sign that said Ibiza on it and tried to hitchhike by the side of the road. This did nobody's mood any good; the holiday spirit and singing of the night before was long gone, even with the instructors' attempts to get the 'Fast Food Song' going.

The boys and girls were absolutely limping with tiredness, and by lunchtime Maggie, who had not slept well at all, couldn't even enjoy the sarcastic remarks about litter picking. She wished with all her heart she could just go home. But then, where even was that now? The school, and her little suite of rooms? With its single bed? Scotland, where accusing faces were on all sides? She thought of the little apartment she and Stan had been so proud of, the painting party all their friends had shown up to, the painting getting increasingly erratic as the six packs had come out, the footie on in the background, so the boys kept not paying attention. It had been simple, then, life.

And now somehow she was picking up old Costa Coffee cups by the side of a road on Dartmoor in the pissing rain, with a so-called boyfriend who couldn't even look her in the eye.

Her mood was unimproved by a dull stew for lunch, and the instructors trying to build up energy for the games that afternoon. They had, after the rather useful split of walkers and kayakers, made the – to Maggie – insane decision of pitting the two schools against each other. But even as she'd mentioned it, Liz, who frankly couldn't believe that you could get a man like David and then not be nice to him, had given her a look and said, 'What, you think we're so inadequate we wouldn't have a chance against your special children?' and Maggie had tried to explain that wasn't what she meant at all, she just wanted them to carry on integrating so nicely, and Liz had said, what, until the Downey lot all went back to their castle, and Maggie's temper flared and it took all her self-control to smile and tell herself that everyone was tired and dirty and sick of communal living.

And certainly, the rivalry put a fire up the children in the afternoon, screaming their heads off at the climbing challenges, the timed rope walks and the bean bag transfers.

David managed to sidle up to her while she was putting a plaster on Duboyce Wang, who, even though he was well over six foot two, was wearing the look of a brave toddler expecting a lollipop at the end of it.

'I'm sorry about last night,' he said. 'I just … it didn't seem right.'

'I agree,' said Maggie brightly. 'It was completely inappropriate. I really do get in the way, don't I? When there's so many more important things to do.'

'Maggie.' David looked pained.

'I think I should probably have some Calpol,' said Duboyce.

'You're fine,' said Maggie and David at the same time.

'Don't worry about me,' said Maggie.

'That's all I do,' said David.

'Nobody is worrying about me,' observed Duboyce, just as they heard raised voices outside.

*

It had happened on the stepladder up to the ropes; two lads jumping at the same time, that was all. It would be, David saw with sinking heart, Bryce and Archie Silver.

'Oi oi,' he said as the two squared up to each other, and did what he had done every other time during his teaching career – walked straight in between them.

'Come on. Calm down, you lot.'

'He thinks he can just push past everyone,' spat Silver.

'I'm terribly sorry. I genuinely didn't see you there.'

'That's because you don't look. You think of nobody and you don't look for anyone.'

'It was a mistake.'

'It wasn't. You think you're entitled to the world.'

'Too right,' said Ismé, who was standing next to Fliss.

'Well, maybe everyone should,' observed Alice.

'Where does that get us?' said Ismé.

'It gets us the world,' said Alice. 'Durr.'

Ismé snorted loudly.

The boys backed off and Mercy wisely called an end to the proceedings, announcing the results as a dead heat – to massed booing from both of the schools – and her smile let everyone know that she was well aware of this discrepancy and happy to soak up the enmity.

'But I thought,' she said, 'I thought you'd want to finish now so you can get ready for the disco. *And* pizza.'

There was quiet.

'Yes, it's ordered-in pizza.'

There was a proper cheer at this, and the girls and boys scattered to their separate huts.

Simone and Calvin walked back to the camp together, as she tried to explain why Mr Micawber in *David Copperfield* (they had moved on to added reading, something which would have astounded David. Simone had pointed out it was a good way to get extra credit; Calvin had secretly listened to it half the night) was technically funny rather than, as he appeared to both of them, genuinely frightening.

'You going to the dance?'

Simone shrugged. 'I think it's compulsory.'

He looked at her, smirking.

'You don't sound so keen.'

'Dancing is not really my thing,' said Simone, pushing up her glasses.

'Oh come on, man! Everyone likes dancing.'

Simone frowned. She absolutely hated dancing, it made her jiggle and she always got red in case anyone was looking at her and then she lost the time and felt really awkward. She never danced.

'No.'

'You'll dance with me.'

'I won't.'

'Come on.'

He smiled his lazy smile.

'Don't be stupid, you don't want to dance with me.'

'Yes I do. You're thick.'

'I know. I hate it.'

'You shouldn't. It's great.'

'I have a boyfriend,' said Simone, blushing bright red.

'Yeah yeah, man,' said the unperturbable Calvin. 'I said a dance, not a ring.'

'I'm sure there's lots of girls who want to dance with you,' stuttered Simone.

'Course there is,' he said, and loped ahead to the boys' quarters. Behind her, Fliss was white-faced with fury.

Chapter Thirty-two

The air in the girls' dormitory block was heavy with the scent of deodorant and hairspray; perfume, cheap and expensive, mingling in a cloud so thick you could choke on it; lots of excited squealing and competitively long eyelashes.

They'd been allowed their phones back for the last night, under strict instructions not to post anything without permission, and everyone was scrolling through and taking a million selfies.

Simone opened hers, and gasped.

Fliss couldn't help herself. Simone had almost no Instagram presence at all, but underneath her last picture, of her parents' restaurant looking pretty on a pink London evening, someone had written 'OH MY GOD THIS LOOKS SO SHIT'.

'What?' said Happy, sitting on the opposite bed.

Simone showed her.

'Wow,' said Happy. 'But you've only got forty followers. How could anyone else have seen it?'

'It's a Korean name and it says they're in Korea,' said Simone, miserable. How could people be so horrible about her parents' little place?

Fliss froze. Simone wouldn't tell anyone. Simone wouldn't realise. She couldn't.

'Korean?' said Alice's languid voice from her own bed.

Fliss's insides turned to iced water.

'I have a super-bitch Korean on mine too, let me see.'

She came over and sat next to Simone.

'Oh my God! It's the same super-bitch!'

They pressed the info page but of course there was no info on Seo-Joon at all.

'Well, we share *none* of the same friends,' said Alice, snottily. 'If someone knows who you are and who I am, it must be through the school. God, I thought it was just some little troll a thousand miles away, not worth noticing, you know? I mean, if their life is really that sad they have to send hate-filled messages to me, God bless them, you know what I mean? I'll just carry on having a good time. But . . . '

Even Alice found it hard to argue with the obviousness that while her lifestyle might attract jealousy and abuse, Simone was completely blameless.

Happy came over, Carey by her side.

'You know,' she said, 'there's a way of finding out where it was posted, tracking it geographically.'

Fliss bit her fingers inside her mouth to stop herself making an involuntary noise.

Simone handed her phone over to Happy, her heart thumping inside her chest. Who? Who would hate her so much? She knew she wasn't popular, but surely that was just because people ignored her – just big Simone who got all the A's. They ignored her because she was a nerd, but surely nobody *hated* her. Her face was a deep miserable red.

'Oh my God!' said Carey, watching Happy's fingers. Her tone was a mixture of shock and gossipy excitement.

'It's coming *from here*!'

'But there's no Korean girls here!' said Alice. 'Min-Lee is Hong Kong Chinese.'

'And very nice,' said Simone.

'It's someone here!' said Alice. 'Pretending to be Korean.'

'That is *so* racist,' said Ismé. The others nodded seriously. Alice looked around the room. Then her eyes fell on someone. She stared straight at her.

'*What?*' said Fliss.

The other girls turned round, painfully slowly.

'Fliss,' said Alice, in a flippant, ice-cold voice, 'can I see your Instagram login?'

Fliss jumped up, hiding her phone behind her.

'Oh my GOD, I can't BELIEVE you would say that! I can't BELIEVE you would think I would do something like that.'

'Well give me your phone then,' said Alice, in that same terrifying tone of voice.

'You can have a look at mine,' said Happy.

'Fuck off!' said Fliss. 'You can't go through people's phones.'

'Here's mine,' said Carey.

'She's probably doing it to herself for attention,' said Fliss.

'Who's "she"?' said Simone, bewildered and miserable.

The whole room was staring at Fliss. She turned round and banged the door on her way out, noisy tears descending.

There was silence in the dorm, broken occasionally by Simone sobbing.

'Oh my God,' said Alice, shaking her head. 'I didn't think it would go that far. Did you?' She turned to Simone.

'I ... I knew she was upset with you. Because you didn't see her in the summer.'

'I was away in the summer!'

'I'm just saying,' said Simone. 'I don't know why she did it to me.'

'Because of Calvin,' said Happy, and Carey nodded.

'What do you mean?'

'Everyone knows you guys have been hanging out loads. Everyone thinks you're going to get it on.'

'Me? And *Calvin*?' Simone was simultaneously horrified and thrilled. 'It would be like me getting off with Harry Styles. *I don't think so.*'

But then she remembered what he had said, and couldn't help but feel a little warm inside.

'I'm just saying what people are saying,' said Happy, politely leaving out the bit where people had expressed varying levels of incredulity.

'And you know she keeps going on about him.'

'*God*, I wish people would stop objectifying black men,' said Ismé.

'They're objectifying good-looking people, Ismé,' said Alice. 'I don't see that stopping anytime soon.'

Ismé harrumphed.

'So she must have got jealous. Oh Christ, she is *such* a baby,' said Alice. She turned again to Simone.

'Was she *really* that upset with me?'

Simone nodded.

'Well, that's exactly why I don't take her to grown-up places! Because she behaves like a child!'

'It's OK to be a child,' said Ismé.

'And I did not say it wasn't, you adultist,' said Alice, always ready. They grinned at each other.

'What are we going to do?' said Simone. 'Should we tell someone?'

The Phillip Dean girls stared at her, absolutely horrified.

'You mean . . . *grass*?' said Patricia.

'No!' said Simone. 'I mean, get her some help.'

'*We* don't grass,' said Carey.

'It's not grassing,' said Simone. 'There's an array of support services and therapists available and . . . '

She saw the PD girls look at her open-mouthed.

'Uh, yeah, you're right. No grassing,' she said.

Fliss cowered in the bathroom, trying to work out how she could run away. She had a credit card for strict emergencies, but she couldn't go home, she was on no-speaks with her parents as it was. In her highly overwrought state she imagined they'd be furious to see her, despite the fact that Caroline had completely forgotten they'd ever fallen out in the first place.

And of course she had no real idea where they were. Plus, the last time she'd run away it had ended very badly indeed. She couldn't do it again, nobody would give a toss. She sobbed hard into her hands. If only she and Hattie didn't hate each other so much, Hattie could have come and picked her up in the car. How stupid. And now she had lost every friend she had ever had. Everyone would find out about it! She'd be a laughing stock. She'd be on everyone's socials. Everybody would hear about her, at every school in Cornwall! She couldn't even go to another school, everyone would know she was the lowest of the low: she had trolled her own best friends.

Fliss sobbed her little heart out.

Chapter Thirty-three

Back in the dorm, the other girls were having a council of war.

'Is she ... does she have issues with her mental health?' said Happy. 'Because we should probably be kind.'

Alice snorted.

'What if Simone had problems with her mental health? She could have ended up in hospital with something like that! What if I gave a shit about it?'

This was undeniable.

'She's a narcissist,' continued Alice, savagely. 'She gets self-obsessed all the time, and totally pass-agg, then she always does shit like this. Do you remember when she fainted at the Christmas party?'

'That wasn't pass-agg,' said Simone mildly. 'She did actually faint.'

'And she fell out with us when she cut her hair because she didn't like it! And when Ismé didn't want to get off with her.'

'Hey, don't bring me into your bs John Lewis problems,' said Ismé.

'Well you are in it,' said Alice. 'Because you go to our school and sleep in our dorm and I know you like to pretend you are still massively off the streets and everything but I have to point out to you that you wear a kilt to school and play field hockey, so you're a Downey girl, I'm afraid.'

'*You're* defending the school?' said Ismé.

There was a silence.

'Should we go look for her?' said Simone, timidly.

'Oh yeah, well done, Fliss, again, getting everyone's attention,' said Alice. 'God no.'

'She did seem really upset.'

Alice covered her head with a pillow.

'God, *please* just get her to get off with someone,' she said. 'It's clearly pure sexual frustration. Honestly. Someone sort her out before she ends up in jail. Ismé, pleeeeasse ...'

'I am not whoring myself to your deranged mate!'

'Fair enough. Well I refuse to believe that with thirty-six lads out there, half of them who go to an all-boys' school, there isn't *one* spotty desperate case that wouldn't take her on.'

Alice folded her arms. Then she unfolded them again and picked up her phone.

'It's been going on for months,' she said, passing round the mean comments on her Insta. 'I'm going to tell people.'

Simone frowned.

'Oh, come *on*!' said Alice. 'She's been awful to you too.'

'I was just thinking,' said Simone, ever diligent, 'isn't it a bit *The Scarlet Letter*?'

'Neh,' said Ismé. 'If she slept with that bloke and we shamed her for it, *that* would be *The Scarlet Letter*.'

'Well,' said Simone, primly, her cheeks growing pink. 'You did that too.'

Ismé looked at her for a long moment, as Simone felt a bit sick, then shrugged.

'Yeah, well,' she said. 'She's just such a *child*.'

'We're all children,' said Simone. 'We're allowed to make mistakes. Aren't we?'

There was silence.

'You mean not tell anyone?' said Carey.

'I don't really know her,' said Happy, shrugging.

'It's up to Alice,' said Ismé. 'She's the one who got the most of this shit.'

'Oh my God,' said Alice. 'I DO! NOT! CARE! Ugh, I cannot believe I am trapped in this madhouse with all of you for another two and a half years. Genuinely cannot believe it. How it doesn't contravene my human rights, I have no idea.'

'Yeah, this really compares to living in a slum in—'

'CAN IT, WOKEZILLA!'

Alice pulled her designer sleeping bag over her head.

Simone went in the end. She couldn't understand, she couldn't imagine doing anything so spiteful. But she could kind of see. A bit. That it was just Fliss's unhappiness. Even though, from Simone's point of view, pretty, petite, rich, blonde Fliss, whose parents fulfilled her every whim, had literally nothing to be unhappy about.

They had, though, agreed to keep it among themselves – at least until they got back to school: they were schoolgirls, not saints.

Fliss's crying wasn't noisy and performative, as it usually was, waiting for someone to come and ask her how she was doing. It was quiet and heart-rending, as deep in misery as a fifteen-year-old can be.

'Everyone hates me,' she said, as Simone put a comforting arm around her shoulders.

'I think everyone is just thinking about what shoes they're going to wear,' said practical Simone, kindly. 'Honestly, it's a one-day wonder.'

'I'm so so sorry,' said Fliss. 'I don't think that about your restaurant at all.'

Simone looked at her. She could feel very insecure about herself, and ashamed of her parents' ways, all the time. But suddenly, as if she was starting to grow up, all of that fell away. It was quite a sudden realisation, and she herself was quite surprised by it.

'I'm proud of my parents,' she said, completely out of the blue. 'They came to this country with absolutely nothing. They worked and worked and worked and worked to make a success of themselves and to give me and Joel a better life. I don't give a shit what you think about it.'

They were both completely flabbergasted by this speech of Simone's. Fliss nodded, swallowing the huge lump in her throat.

'Good,' she said, humbled.

'Come on,' said Simone, bravely. 'Let's get you to this dance.'

'I'm not going to the sodding dance.'

'It's obligatory,' said Simone.

'OK,' said Fliss, washing her face. She sighed at her pinched reflection in the mirror, red and blotchy.

'Oh God, I look nine.'

'Who cares?' said Simone, on a roll.

'OK,' said Fliss. 'Does Alice hate me?' Then she shrugged. 'She didn't care about me before, I don't think it will have changed very much.'

'There you go then,' said Simone.

Fliss took a deep breath.

'And you're really not going to tell people?'

Simone shook her head.

'I think,' she said, 'being a teenager is hard enough, don't you?'

Fliss nodded.

'I am so so so so sorr—'

'Yeah, all right.'

'I'm going to take a bit of a walk outside, clear my head, is that OK? I'll come to the dance.'

Simone nodded, and watched her go. Then she followed her. Just in case.

Chapter Thirty-four

The rain had stopped, and a weak setting sun was descending in a watery sky over Dartmoor. Inside, however, the rec room, with its old board games and scruffy stacking chairs, had been given as much of a disco makeover as could be managed; there was a small light-rack sending out colours, and a disco ball with many of its mirror bits missing. But the doors were open to the outside, and the insects were circling lazily, and 'Get Lucky' was playing at high volume, and there was a small table set up with soft drinks and crisps and chocolate bars, and the smell of Lynx deodorant and perfume, cheap and expensive, was heavy on the air, overshadowing at last the heavy aroma of tarpaulin and wellie boot socks, so it was practically exotic. The groups of children came in, sniggering, nudging each other.

The Downey girls all looked the same. They were wearing tight jeans and crop tops, showing off little tummies; sexy, but modest at the same time. The Phillip Dean girls looked incredible. Bright minidresses; cut-out shapes on frocks; every colour (the Downey girls stuck to blacks and pinks); eyebrow-raising hotpants and bralet tops. David had seen it before at their school discos and had learned basically just to keep his eyes on the back wall; he assumed the boys were used to it.

The Downey boys weren't though. They looked like they were in a gigantic tin of Quality Street. Maggie was happy to see the girls. She liked the showing-out girls, they reminded her of being younger, back in Glasgow, although she hadn't ever gone quite this far. Even so, the make-up larded on with a trowel, the laminated brows, the startled gigantic spiders of the stick-on eyelashes; they didn't look like the fresh-faced girls they were; they looked like terrifying women who could be any age between twenty and fifty, plastered in contoured foundation, with exaggerated lips practically touching the bottom of their nostrils; all their normal nerviness obliterated in the sheer weight of Fenty and Rimmel. Maggie felt nothing but affection for them, and checked the Downey girls, to make sure they weren't sneering. They seemed as impressed as the boys, however, filled with questions as to how they did their make-up and keen to strike up complicated conversations about Pretty Little Thing and Klarna.

Meanwhile, the Phillip Dean boys were late. Archie Silver had, somehow, got his paws on a smuggled bottle of cheap whisky and they were handing it round the back of the building, quickly swigging down the revolting fiery stuff before they got discovered. They only emerged when the pizzas arrived, to massive cheers from the students, already noisy and larking around, though not noticeably more than they normally might.

The kids fell on the pizza and Maggie hung back at the end, making sure, as she habitually did, that Fliss was eating hers. Except Fliss wasn't there. Maggie frowned. Oh, surely not. Fliss was always getting into trouble. Please, please let there not be any more.

She glanced around. Who was in that room? The dorm, plus four PD students. She glanced up. There was no sign of Simone either, nor Alice, although she hadn't really been expecting Alice.

Maggie sighed. Where there was trouble, she could always search for her own home class.

David approached her, still completely aware of how desperately they had to talk; the gulf that was opening between them that he felt powerless to bridge.

'Hey,' he said, spotting her grim face. 'What's up?'

'It's my utterly bloody S4s again.'

Maggie had never quite lost the habit of referring to her pupils by their Scottish year-groups. She meant the year elevens, but David always understood.

'They are quite the challenge,' he said. 'Who is it now?'

'Fliss isn't here.' Maggie frowned. 'She's not meant to miss a meal. I'd better go find her.'

He nodded. Maggie waited for him to say something, anything – the children were busy with pizza or eyeing up each other – but he didn't.

'OK then,' she said, heading for the door, fuming.

'Maggie,' he said, indicating the room. He knew she was upset about last night but they simply couldn't have it out now. 'You *know* I can't ... that it isn't ... can we talk once we're out of here?'

Maggie shrugged.

'Whatever,' she said, in exactly the same way as his year elevens did. He smiled to himself, mirthlessly.

Away from the buildings, up in the treeline, it was getting dark and gloomy. The music still pounded away though, in a place where there were no neighbours to get ratty about it; no parents to shout that it needed turning down and no school rules that forbade it, and nobody tutting or giving them looks for playing music out loud on the bus, and the kids had managed to discuss with Klay, youngest and cool-est (albeit a very relative term to the kids) member of the Outward Bound support staff, which records they could play and whether 'WAP' was allowed (it manifestly was not) and whether Jason Derulo was, if they did the radio edits (yes).

But they had now abseiled in front of each other; fallen in the water; worn wildly unflattering tracksuits; picked up rubbish. They weren't as inhibited as they would be at school or at home. The dancing started almost right away; huge circles of girls, from all worlds, as the boys teased each other and jostled against the walls, trying to gauge their moments for joining the girls without making idiots of themselves.

Simone got further and further away from the building, where all the fun was. Typical, she thought to herself. All the normal people out enjoying themselves normally.

But she couldn't leave Fliss roaming about completely on her own. Alice didn't care – Alice didn't care about anything. But soft-hearted Simone marched on. She knew she wasn't Fliss's first choice of friend. But at the moment, she was all she had.

'Fliss!' she shouted.

'Oi,' came a voice suddenly, gentle in the gloom. She shot round. There was Calvin, tall in the twilight. 'You all right?'

Simone shrugged.

'Oh yeah, I'm fine.'

'What are you doing out here? Are you not going to go to the disco?'

His dark eyes were full of concern.

'Yes! I'm not that much of a nerd, thank you!'

'I didn't mean it like that,' he said, clearly meaning it like that.

'It's my friend Fliss.'

She thought about what had made Fliss so unhappy, so left it out; it wasn't just Alice, she knew.

'Actually,' said Simone, almost without thinking, 'it's kind of about you.'

'*Me?* How come?'

'I think she likes you.'

'Oh. Yeah,' said Calvin.

Simone laughed. 'You are not in the least bit surprised! Does everyone like you?'

He smiled.

'Not *everyone*.'

'Oh my God, they do. You are so up yourself.'

Calvin allowed himself a private smile. 'Come on, I can barely read. You have to give me my ways with the ladies. Except you.'

Simone smiled to herself, she couldn't help it.

'You can read absolutely bloody fine,' she said. 'That's why you're going to read those Cliffs Notes before you go back to school.'

'Mr McDonald is going to be amazed.'

Simone shook her head. 'He won't. He'll feel vindicated.'

'What does that mean?'

'It means he was right all along.'

'Huh,' said Calvin, pleased. 'So hang on, which girl is this?'

'The thin one with the short hair.'

'Oh,' said Calvin. He frowned.

'So . . . ' Simone coloured a little, but was determined to go ahead. 'I was going to ask you a favour.'

'I'm not getting off with your mate, man! Don't pimp me!'

Simone burst out laughing.

'Oh my God, you massive weirdo! But I was going to ask. Could you maybe walk her in to the disco? She's all right

200

really. Just had a tough time of it with the other girls ... Girl stuff ... it can be bad.'

'You are trying to pimp me!'

'I'm ... a teeny-tiny bit. I'll proofread your essay.'

'Oh come on.'

'What do you need to get your scholarship anyway?'

'Sixes,' said Calvin bitterly, as if the answer was 'To fly to the moon.'

Simone, to her credit, did not laugh. The GCSE marks went from 9–1, 9 being the best.

'You can get a six,' she said, 'if I help you.'

'Seriously?' He weighed it up. 'Seriously, Sims. Will I be OK at the school?'

Simone paused in the moonlight, pushing back her glasses.

'I don't know,' she said. 'Although I think everyone likes you already. But whatever you feel like when you're there, you might do better after. Even if you hate it. Just for going, you get more chances. That's the deal.'

He snorted. 'It's not a fair deal.'

'It isn't,' said Simone.

They walked on.

'This mate of yours ... she's not, like, a neo-Nazi or anything? I'm not going to find TikToks of her using the "n" word or nothing?'

'No,' said Simone. 'She just ... she just finds things difficult, that's all.'

'Yeah, I've heard that about skinny white blonde chicks,' sniffed Calvin. 'Yeah. OK. Deal. Look at my essay, OK?'

Fliss had run up into the woods, away from it all. She was sure everything would have got around the other kids by now, whatever Simone said. They'd all know she was a pathetic basement-dwelling troll. Worse, a catfisher, and even

201

worse, someone who'd culturally appropriated another race. Oh my God. How could she have been so stupid? How could she have been so dumb? Tears of absolute bitter regret ran down her face.

She came across a clearing in the wood where somebody had hung a wooden swing from a tall tree. The rising moon shone through the rustling branches; it was rather lovely, and suited her very dramatic mood. She sat on it and started to swing, leaning her head against the old twisted rope and wondering what, exactly, to do.

In fact, bustling into the hall, the girls weren't giving Fliss a second thought. There was so much else to think about: the music, the lights, how they would look when dancing and whether there was enough vegan pizza left for Ismé.

Maggie had caught up with them at the doorway.

'Where's Fliss?' she said suspiciously. Alice gave her most innocent look.

'Oh, she's just taking the air,' she said. 'She'll be along presently.'

'"Presently",' whispered Ismé, laughing, and Alice gave her the Vs, so situation more or less normal, thought Maggie. She watched them head in, chattering, and would have gone in too, except she was feeling slightly awkward at having just stormed away from David and wasn't crazy to have to crawl back.

This was solved by David appearing in front of her. Everyone else was inside, and the rousing chorus of 'Uptown Funk' appeared to be meeting with general approval.

'Are you OK?' he said, trying to get through to her. 'Can you tell me what's up?'

'What's up with *me*?' said Maggie. She was hissing, trying to keep her voice low. 'What's up with *you*? You haven't said a single word to me the entire time we've been here. Every time I walk in a room you walk out of it!'

'We talked about this,' said David, looking perplexed. 'To keep apart in front of the children.'

'They're not children! They're all twerking in there! And they all know, and none of them give a stuff, so you could at least probably sit next to me from time to time. And last night! When you were supposedly *so desperate* to see me!!'

David let out a groan.

'Oh, Maggie. What could I possibly have done last night? It was completely impossible from the second I stepped into the boat. There was a lot going on with the boys, and we're all sharing bedrooms, for goodness' sake. It's unprofessional, inappropriate, and if we got caught, I would never work in teaching again.'

'As if Phillip Dean would sack you,' said Maggie.

'What's that supposed to mean?' said David, bristling. 'It's got the potential to be a great school.'

'Can! We! STOP! TALKING! ABOUT! SCHOOL!'

There was silence.

'There's ... I wanted to talk to you,' said David. 'But this didn't feel like the right place.'

'Talk to me about what?' said Maggie, panicked. She knew it. Her family had been so cool towards him. He hadn't enjoyed Christmas at all, she'd known. He thought she was low class and demanding, and he was going to break up with her. Of course.

'Nothing ... I mean ... ' He raised his hands, as Silver and his friends disappeared out behind the huts again, sniggering with one another.

'Oh lord,' he said. 'That looks like trouble. I'd better check it out.'

'Course you should,' said Maggie, turning away.

'Maggie, please. PLEASE. Can it just wait till we're home?'

'Absolutely,' said Maggie. 'Just make sure you put me absolutely last on your agenda.'

From behind the huts came the sound of smashing glass and a distinctive whiff of tobacco.

'Maggie!'

Chapter Thirty-five

'Hey.'

Fliss looked up. She had got quite carried away with the sense of herself as a lonely abandoned maiden, under the moon, and while she was half-expecting a voice, she'd assumed it would be Simone, making sure she wasn't doing anything stupid, as ever.

In fact, Simone was a better friend to Fliss than she could ever have imagined, or even deserved, and as handsome Calvin walked into the glade, Fliss's heart lit up straight away.

'What are you doing up here?'

Simone was walking away, feeling oddly regretful. Obviously she had a boyfriend but ... and she didn't fancy Calvin, not really. He was more like a sweet big brother ... but he had seen her. He had liked her. She hugged herself.

In the glade, Calvin shrugged.

'Not much. What are you doing?'

Fliss sighed melodramatically.

'Oh. Everybody hates me.'

'What did you do?'

'Stupid stuff. Really stupid. Really, really stupid and awful.'

She dissolved into tears again, pouring over her hands. Calvin shifted uncomfortably.

'Oh man, what did you do? What did you do?'

He was genuinely concerned; the girl was in such distress, shaking and sobbing.

'Did someone take a video of you? Are they saying things about you? Did some geezer do something to you?'

She shook her head, helplessly, unable to speak.

'Because if they did, man, we'll sort them out ...'

'No, no,' whispered Fliss, eventually. 'It's not like that.'

'Is it your family? Is something up with them?'

'NO ... no ...'

Finally she pulled it together.

'I wrote mean comments on someone's 'gram.'

Calvin stared at her.

'And?'

'And ... I pretended to be Korean!'

This brought on a fresh burst of sobbing. Calvin bit his lip and waited to hear more. One of his best mates had got beaten up in a fracas outside a police van for stealing a vape. That guy had problems.

'Uh, that's it?'

Fliss's head was back in her arms again and she nodded piteously.

'Well, are you sorry you done it?'

'Yes.'

'Good. Fine. Say sorry then.'

'You think I'm being stupid.'

'Everyone's got problems, man.'

'I don't think I'm a bad person. But I keep getting everything wrong.'

Calvin smiled, but not unkindly.

'Maybe because you got given ... so much stuff at birth. You're swimming in it.'

'What?'

'I dunno, man. Privilege, all that stuff. You're . . . you're like a fish trying to figure out what the birds are doing.'

'But it's so hard.'

'Yes,' said Calvin. 'Now you're getting it. Other people have it tough.'

'I know,' said Fliss. 'But I didn't make it that way.'

'You didn't,' said Calvin. 'But we all have to start changing it.'

Fliss eyed him up.

'Why are you failing school?' she said. 'You're really really smart.'

'And you're looking at me from the fishbowl, not the sky.'

'Well, I still think you should come to our school.'

The strains of Drake came meandering up the hillside.

'Come on,' he said. 'Wanna go?'

Fliss made a sharp intake of breath. He couldn't mean it.

'With . . . with you?'

Calvin shrugged.

'If you like.'

Chapter Thirty-six

Round the back of the dance hall, the kids had dispersed and there was nothing to be seen, just a faint whiff of smoke on the air, and distant laughter. David cursed. He had to keep an eye on the children, and this thing with Maggie seemed to be spiralling out of control. Was it her way, he thought, of gently ending it? Of breaking the dream, of moving further and further away?

He walked back into the hall, full now with the scent of perfume and hairspray and trainers. The children were making full use of their phones, taking videos and photos of everything in sight, with the fervour of people believing they would never see each other again. Instagram posts were discussed, even without a signal, and planned: hearting was promised and debated by the girls and they pored over the photos until they had each found a filter they were happy with. The dancers were mixing, between schools, boys and girls, everyone enjoying the feel of their bodies; the open air, the euphoria of being away from normal life, from the pressures of the forthcoming exams – nobody had opened a book the entire time they'd been there, Calvin technically excepted.

The sheer joy of being young, and dancing, meant the noise levels were insane. David glanced around for Simone, normally hugging the walls at these things, but she was absent too. She must be comforting Fliss, he thought, and Maggie must have gone to find them.

He looked somewhat worriedly up at the far corner, where the lights didn't reach, and it was dark. Bryce and Kelisa were dancing together or, more precisely, grinding. He checked with Mercy, who nodded to say she was aware of the situation.

Silver and his cronies, meanwhile, had re-entered the room, giggling and nudging each other, and falling over. David wanted to go find Maggie, but he couldn't; not if it looked like things might get a bit complicated. A little bit of horseplay was unavoidable with this many fifteen- and sixteen-year-olds in one place; drunkenness or sex absolutely wasn't. He wished he'd picked up his phone, but then that might make things even worse.

He helped himself to a glass of cola, which he disliked at the best of times, and winced as it stuck to his teeth To work.

Rihanna was playing as the door opened and the people nearest to it stopped dancing; the quietness spread as the entire room stopped to see what was happening.

Fliss was beaming, her normally pinched, worried face pink and pretty; her hair, now, at least long enough to cram under a rather cute headband; her crop top, in line with every other Downey girl's, a rather fetching soft pink that went well with Calvin's long white T-shirt, his arm draped casually around her shoulders. Maggie, stalking off to bed, had seen them coming down the hill together, side by side not arm in arm, and had been pleasantly surprised; then more perplexed when they stopped outside the doorway and Calvin had offered to put his arm around her.

'Oh, *thank God*,' said Alice, in genuine pleasure. Ismé rolled

209

her eyes. Happy, Patricia and Carey were genuinely pleased for her too; at least she'd stopped crying. Fliss could see they weren't hostile when she came in, and the DJ changed the music to 'Never Enough' from *The Greatest Showman*, a signal, well understood, for the coupled-up to slow dance, and the unaccompanied girls to sing along at the top of their lungs.

Even more amazingly, Calvin took Fliss in his arms, and Simone, slipping in unnoticed just a few seconds later, thought two things; one that this was going above and beyond what she'd asked for, and two, what a rather lovely couple they made.

She happily reclaimed her confiscated phone, expecting to find a dozen long and strongly worded emails from Ash on how terrible his life was without her, which she did.

Feeling a bit guilty about the whole Calvin thing – nothing had happened, she told herself, she'd just liked him, that was all – she helped herself to several bars of chocolate and a large Coke, took herself off up the hill to get a signal to download the emails, then went to her dorm to have a bit of time to herself, and talk to her boyfriend. As a result she missed the whole thing.

Everyone was so distracted – some jealously, some just interested in the gossip – that they weren't looking to see what was happening in the dark corner at the back of the hall. Bryce had gone in for the kill, and had his hand on Kelisa's waist. She was getting close to him. Silver and his mates were full of cheap cider and hormones, and instantly checked it out.

'Oi!' shouted Silver. 'Get off her.'

'I *beg* your pardon?' said Bryce, turning around and pulling himself up to his full height, dwarfing Silver. 'This is none of your fucking business.'

'YEAH,' shouted Kelisa, but nonetheless she pulled up her slipping silver strapless dress and hurried out from behind him.

Bryce stared down his nose at Silver and said in his most imperious voice, 'Fully consensual, mate. That's a word of more than one syllable, so if you need me to explain it to you—'

Silver needed nothing explaining to him. And he also had something Bryce had never had: plenty of street-fighting experience, as well as a gutful of cider. He pulled back his fist, and punched Bryce full in the nuts.

Within two seconds there was pandemonium. Bryce was under a large group of boys, Kelisa started screaming her head off, and the other girls were joining in, unprompted.

David rushed up, again, throwing himself into the fray; Nicholas Craig was rather slower off the mark, but did come over. Mrs Offili got the music switched off and the lights up, which broke the spell of the evening immediately. Once again, they were children, in a scruffy rec room with fire exit signs everywhere; battered old chairs, scuffed wooden floor and the smell of a school cafeteria. The magic of being sixteen on a warm and moonlit night faded away. Fliss felt utter disappointment as Calvin stepped away from her. Alice didn't look up from where she was busy making sure she didn't appear in anyone's Instagram photographs.

Together with two of the young instructors, they got hold of a pinwheeling Silver, who was spitting and cursing at the top of his lungs. Bryce was doubled over, clutching himself and shouting something about his mother being a QC. None of the Downey boys seemed willing to get further involved in fighting; plenty of the PD boys looked well up for it.

David looked at Nicholas to see if he was going to do

anything, but obviously he wasn't. He grabbed Silver by the collar of his jacket, and beckoned Bryce.

'Right, the two of you. With me. How drunk are you?' he said to Silver. 'Are you going to throw up?'

'I'm going to throw up on *him*,' snarled Silver.

'Fine. I'm going to stick you in a toilet by yourself till you've sobered up.'

'I'm fine,' said Silver.

'Can I let go of you?'

'I'm fine.'

'Guttersnipe,' said Bryce, not remotely under his breath. 'Yes. I need to see you. I'm filing charges.'

Mercy bade them follow her to her office, which was covered in maps, camping gear, boots and brightly coloured brochures.

'OK,' she said. 'Do we need the police?'

'Yes,' said Bryce immediately. Silver looked at him.

'Grass,' he said.

'Are you all right?' said David. 'Do you want someone to take a look at you?'

Bryce shook his head quickly.

'I'm fine, thanks. Despite an unprovoked attack.'

'You went for her!' said Silver. 'You perv.'

'She was perfectly willing.'

David looked at Mercy. 'Liz has got her,' she said.

'For God's sake,' said David to Bryce. 'Of all the girls here.'

'She was chatting me up!'

'After what happened!'

He shrugged.

'I'll have you,' yelled Silver.

David sighed.

'I do not want to call the police out for nonsense,' he said. 'Silver, that was ridiculously stupid what you did.'

212

'Ridiculous? It was criminal what he did!' said Bryce, taking out his phone. 'I'm calling my father.'

'And you,' said David, 'you want to walk into the merest rumour of impropriety and have it hanging over your head while everyone writes your college admission letters, go right ahead.'

'*What?*' said Bryce. 'How's that fair?'

'You took advantage of a girl you already knew to be vulnerable who you had already been warned to stay away from,' said Mercy.

Bryce blinked.

'But she . . . '

'If I hear that one more time,' said the normally completely unflappable Mercy, 'I'm going to punch you in your entitled bollocks yourself.'

'Right, bed,' said David to Silver. 'You're missing the rest of the night. Any more nonsense and you're in serious trouble, do you hear me? If we weren't going home in the morning, I'd send you both home now.'

Silver nodded.

Then he looked up at Bryce.

'I'm not sorry I stopped you from Kelisa,' he muttered. 'That girl has shit in her life you have no idea. But I shouldn't have punched you in the bollocks. Sorry.'

There was a long silence.

Finally, Bryce's shoulders slumped.

'That was . . . ' he said. 'That was the first time I've kissed a real girl.'

There was silence in the room.

Silver boggled at him.

'But . . . you're sixteen, aren't you?'

Bryce shrugged.

'And you're rich and that . . . '

213

'You don't know what it's like!' burst out Bryce. 'Stuck away in the middle of nowhere at that bloody school. I never meet a girl, apart from my sister's friends, and they're nine.'

'What about the Downey girls?' said Silver, still aghast. 'They're a bit stuck-up, but they're all right when you get to know them.'

'Are you kidding? They want blokes with cars, not schoolboys. And anyway, they'd probably kill us.'

'But our girls are fair game?'

'No, but ... I just wanted ... I so wanted ...'

David shook his head in disbelief. When had things got so complicated?

'That's not how you get girls, mate. Lunging in the dark,' said Silver, as if he were thirty-five. 'Or, even if you do, and OK, right, I see now, you probably would with Kelisa, but come on. It was shady, mate.'

'But *how*?'

Silver shrugged. 'Just be nice to them. Be funny. Sweet. Normal stuff. You know?'

'I don't know,' said Bryce sadly.

'You want to get them enthusiastic. Right, here's an idea. You know girls like reality shows? Well, you have to watch them, all right.'

'Aren't they awful?'

'That doesn't matter, it's just nice when you get something they like. You just have to find something ... you know. They like dogs and cats and stuff. So. Ask them about pets. It's not rocket science.'

David looked at Mercy.

'OK, bed, the two of you.'

The two boys wandered off together, Bryce still asking a million questions.

'What are you going to do with them?'

'I'm not sure,' said David. 'Rusticate him, for sure. But it's just so messed up.'

'I would not be a teenager again for a million pounds,' said Mercy.

'Really? An actual million? Your electricity bill is obviously lower than mine.'

'OK. Maybe two million.'

Back in the rec room, the night was over, the strip lights showing the dust in the corners of the room, the mops and buckets in the coat closet, the running mascara and sweated-off skin glitter. The children were tired and although they made an attempt at complaining, were on the whole happy to slope back off to bed to examine their Instagram and follow all their new friends, if they could ever get a signal.

Mercy came back and found Kelisa surrounded by her praetorian guard, and bore her off to the same office, for tea and a long chat about Mercy's own, extremely difficult, upbringing, which Kelisa never forgot.

Meanwhile, Maggie waited for David, but still he did not come.

'I can't believe you put yourself through all that trouble for Mr McDonald and look at you now,' said Miss Starling, who had brassily been following their lack of connection. She was unzipping her toiletries case. 'Well! Just goes to show. Nothing good comes of losing your head.'

Maggie smiled tightly and wished with all her heart that it was the next day and she could leave. One more night. One more night to get through.

She heard the girls trooping in, chattering away, even though it was barely ten o'clock. She supposed she'd better go and count them back in.

She made her tour of the dorms, smiled at the chattering

215

and the discarded frocks and dresses; the assignations, the dancing boys all dissected a million times, the texts, the likes. The boys, she knew, would probably be snoring by now.

There was no sign of Fliss. Maggie sighed. Oh goodness. Please let her not be up to anything ridiculous in the woods with that big handsome Phillip Dean lad.

In the forest clearing, just away from the dorms, Calvin was smiling.

'I need to go, they've already killed one boy for kissing tonight.'

'I know,' said Fliss, her heart beating a million miles an hour. 'I just . . . '

'What?'

Fliss shrugged. Then, in a tiny voice, 'I just . . . nobody ever kissed me goodnight before.'

He looked at her. 'Seerz?'

She shrugged.

'It doesn't matter,' she said, her voice breaking a little bit. Overhead, an owl twitted and the moon glowed.

'Are you holding out for someone special?' he said.

'No,' said Fliss. 'I just wanted . . . somebody nice . . . '

'I'm *quite* nice,' said Calvin, who had enjoyed the dancing and the feel of her in his arms more than he had expected.

'You're very nice!' Her voice was low. 'I would have liked to kiss you, actually.'

He quickly looked around, made sure there was nobody about. Then he reached down and gave Fliss her very first proper, adult kiss in the warm spring air, gently, but strong too, in the middle of the countryside, under a wild white moon. And the worst day of her life turned into the best.

Chapter Thirty-seven

Maggie was sure she would be too irritated and sad to sleep, but it was very late when she got startled awake by something, forgetting for a moment where she was. Then she realised and sat up, wondering what had woken her. Fliss had come in just as she was returning to her dorm, looking flushed and happy and absolutely full of something, and the hushed screaming that came down the corridor as she re-entered her dorm room seemed to back up that belief. Maggie smiled. God. Even Fliss, who could be guaranteed to overthink every given situation, was having a good evening.

She didn't know what had woken her now though and sat up. There it came again; a tiny ping at the window. Miss Starling sniffled and shifted over in her bed.

Maggie got up and crept to the window. The moon was so bright it looked like day outside. There was only the rustle of the wind to be heard.

Ping.

The sound came again. She glanced down and realised it was a pebble, expertly hitting her window. Frowning, she leaned over and caught a glimpse, in the moonlight, of David, poking his dark head up from behind a wall, the shadow that had to be Stephen Dedalus skulking behind him.

'*Ssh*,' she mimed at him, as he beamed manically to see her.

And in an instant, all the irritation, all the worry about their future, all the disappointment she'd felt . . . it all vanished, in the hit of pure adrenalin that raced through her.

She glanced at the snorting Miss Starling then, as quietly as she was able, sneaked out into the corridor. There was CCTV and a million dire warnings to the girls that they weren't allowed to leave the property at night-time at risk of instant suspension.

Maggie decided to take her chances. She gently opened the door, praying that it wasn't alarmed – and slipped outside in her pyjamas into the chill spring air.

The grass was damp under her feet, as she darted behind the wall, giggling, and hushing, and falling into his arms.

'You are so mad,' she said. 'We'll get into so much trouble.'

'Ssh,' he said. 'Crawl. Until we're away from the buildings.'

'You are kidding me?'

'Nope. Mercy is pretty tough.'

Maggie thought again of the awfulness of being discovered.

'OK,' she said. 'This is very muddy.'

'You're right,' said David as they crawled along, hysterical with laughter. 'You should take those clothes off, if anything.'

'I will absolutely not be doing that,' said Maggie, giggling, delighted. 'This is a very highly rated place. They probably have dogs and searchlights and barbed wire.'

Once they hit the tree line, they straightened up, weak from laughing.

'You have my attention,' said Maggie. David said nothing. He just put out his hand.

'I didn't realise,' said David, 'how complicated it would be.'

He told her the full story of Bryce and Silver, and her eyes widened.

'Goodness,' she said.

'I'm just conscious,' said David, 'that I don't ... . I don't want to set a bad example to the boys. Being unable to control myself or something.'

There was a pause.

'Apart from now, obviously.'

They wandered on up the hill, an owl hooting; a sense of scurrying in the bracken; small creatures surprised at being disturbed in their own little corners of the universe, the wood, that went on, building nests, digging holes, hiding nuts, climbing trees, eating mushrooms; field mice, dormice, squirrels, starlings, ravens, adders, wood lice, foxes all carried on regardless of the whims and concerns of the two-legged creatures who occasionally strolled among them.

Maggie grew slightly worried.

'So why are you taking the risk *now*?' she said, suddenly terrified he was going to break up with her and couldn't wait a second longer.

'I needed to tell you something,' he said. 'And it can't wait. It can't. I won't ... tomorrow we'll all go back to normal lives and you'll be away all the bloody week at school, and I'll be marking and it's exam season so all hell will break loose and I won't get a chance to see you properly and if I don't say it ... if I don't say it, if I don't know ... '

He tailed off, just as they reached the swing at the top of the hill. It was a large plank of wood, more than big enough for two, and they sat on it without question.

Maggie looked at the ground, kicking her bare feet to make them gently sway back and forwards. He sat next to her, then thought better of it, and stood up.

'Stop swinging,' he said. 'I can't concentrate.'

Maggie frowned and stopped the swing with her foot, looking up at him, his normally mobile face still and concentrated.

Stephen Dedalus came up and put his head under her arm and she skritched his ears instinctively. David saw her do it. Goodness. This wasn't going to make it any easier.

'I realise . . . ' he started. 'I realise that I am not what your family hoped for for you. I'm not sure I'm even what you would have hoped for yourself. But I just . . . I had to let you know. Because I know we don't always get the chance to be together. And I know you have had a tough year. But . . . '

Maggie looked at him, her heart hammering. What was he doing? Was this it? A moonlight glade . . . a full moon. A beautiful, bosky evening. Was he about to get down on one knee? Oh my goodness!

She remembered when Stan had proposed, in the restaurant. And he had been so anxious and it had gone so badly wrong. But she'd been happy, hadn't she? Had she? She could hardly remember.

David saw her worried face.

'What's the matter?'

'I just . . . I mean, what are you doing?'

He frowned. 'Trying to show you how much you mean to me.'

Maggie looked at him expectantly, while trying to smooth out her hair, and he suddenly realised with a clang what she thought he meant. But they'd only been dating for such a short time! And Miranda had barely sent back his stuff from her immaculate, very pastel flat! It was . . . Oh no. He realised he'd muffed it.

'Well?' said Maggie, smiling bravely while being slightly terrified. She hardly knew him.

'Uhm,' he said. 'Well. You do. Mean a lot to me. And. Uh.'

He had never felt more English in his entire life. This is what had driven Miranda crazy – his timidity, his inability to say what he was truly feeling.

Maggie's heart threatened to leap out of her chest. She'd brought some pretty nightwear, just in case, but had abandoned it for her old super-comfy grey jammies, which was annoying in itself. When she'd dared to dream about it, it had always been abroad somewhere, maybe at sunset. Or at Reuben's, perhaps, their secret getaway. Not in a muddy copse on a school trip.

She moved towards him slightly.

'Yes?' she said softly, absolutely not sure what she was going to say.

'Ah, I wondered if ...'

It crossed his mind that, after all, he was nuts about her. After all, would it be the worst thing? After all, did he think he would love someone as much as he loved her, her grey eyes wide as a faun's, her red hair haloing her face? Might it, seeing as he had already got this far, not just be sensible to carry on?

'I wondered if—'

'SIR! SIR! PRINGLE MINOR HAS WET THE BED!'

'I HAVE NOT! MY, UH, MY WATER BOTTLE SPILT!'

They sprang apart, both relieved; both noticing the other person was relieved.

'Will it keep?' said Maggie, quietly.

'I think so,' he said, holding her gaze, before turning and heading back to the children.

Chapter Thirty-eight

Maggie didn't sleep at all, trying to work out what had happened, but her quietness went unremarked the next morning, in the hustle and bustle of gathering together all kit, returning wellies and waterproofs, preparing to head home; most of the kids were excited to be getting back to their normal lives, seeing their families – for even the Downey children only had a couple of weeks to go before the Easter break.

One or two from each school were blatantly not looking forward to going home at all. It made Maggie sad to see it, but she understood completely how they were feeling. She glanced at her watch – 8 a.m.

The children were starting to get loaded onto the coaches. In other circumstances, she would have been genuinely pleased and proud to see the hugs, the high fives, the handles passing between the Downey pupils and the PDs.

Fliss and Calvin had taken their farewells just outside the breakfast room that morning.

'I'll see you?' said Calvin, in his usual laid-back way. 'I mean, if I come to the school, yeah?'

Fliss smiled at him. Now she'd got to know him a bit, he wasn't some huge out-of-reach romantic figure; neither was he some kind of bragging right. He was just a big, sweet, doofusy guy, just like a lot of others. And whether she ever saw him again or not, it didn't matter, she knew, because her memories of her very first kiss, with the best-looking, most popular boy in year eleven, were always going to be happy ones.

'Are we really going to meet up?' said Carey and Happy to Simone.

'Of course!' said Simone. 'Reuben's, next week? They do an ice cream float happy hour.'

The girls grinned, and Simone smiled to herself too.

'All right, Miss Party Animal,' said Alice. 'Let's get on this revolting "coach" then.' She sighed. 'Only three more weeks and I will be in Gstaad. Thank *Christ*.'

Chapter Thirty-nine

The next two weeks passed in a blur. Now the break from classwork was done, the emphasis was all on revision revision revision, to make sure the girls were as ready as they could possibly be for their GCSEs; study sessions in the evenings, drop-ins every lunchtime and break. It seemed a lot to Maggie, always did – at her old school they'd pretty much left the pupils to it – but great results as well as a good environment was what got children through the door at Downey, and the world got more competitive all the time.

David's work was even harder; trying to track down students who hadn't turned in course work, who had stopped coming to class and who had never sat a past paper in their lives. He was determined, absolutely determined, to double the percentage of his students' decent grades from 8 per cent in the last full year before he came. He sat up night after night persuading students to try and write their essays again and again; drilling them on their quotes; trying to spark their imaginations with the creative essay, to get them to pour out their experiences – particularly the children who had come to the country fresh, who remembered their lives before – onto the page, as clearly and vividly as possible. He was barely sleeping, still up providing breakfast in his home room for children who didn't even have a bowl of porridge to wake up to in the morning; marking, re-marking, trying to get them up all the time.

Simone and Calvin were talking online constantly, as she guided him through the book; they watched the films together on Twitch, and he astonished David by how lucidly he could compare his own experiences to young Pip. He was genuinely starting to hope, especially after Mr Craig's uninspiring behaviour at the Outward Bound had left him somewhat in David's debt, and he was indeed looking seriously at the sports scholarships.

Dr Deveral was watching all of this with some interest. The outreach project had tested well with potential parents, particularly the awkward liberal middle-class ones who felt guilty for even considering single-sex boarding schools at all, especially these days. To know that another school was benefiting from the beautiful facilities and acres of green space, the huge swimming pool, the fresh air, the theatre – well, it helped set their minds at rest.

Maggie had stared at him. Neither of them had referred at all to what had happened on the camp. She had gone over it and over it in her head. All she could think was that he had been going to propose, then had, for whatever reason, lost his nerve, or changed his mind. It had completely shattered her. She didn't know where she stood; could not forget that she had given up everything for him. But he was emotionally frozen. The fact that David was a man out of time had always, always been part of the attraction. She loved that about him. But then sometimes he played the starchy Englishman too long, and she couldn't get what he meant at all. Apart from the fact that he was very clearly not proposing to her. That he'd looked at her, and changed his mind.

She thought she'd suggest getting away in the Easter break, once and for all, only to hit a brick wall immediately.

'You're not taking a holiday *at all*?'

David was stubborn.

'I can't,' he said. 'Not if we're going to get these results. I'm running a catch-up school.'

'But nobody will come to that!'

'Do you think that? Is that what you think of my kids?'

Maggie pouted. 'No, of course not. Oh God, don't you want a break from school?'

'This is the last push,' he said. 'I'm just running a revision school. Why don't you come in and help?'

'Because I'm not insured to be on school grounds,' pointed out Maggie, truthfully. 'And I can't stay at Downey House, they're doing some stupid conference and need all the rooms. I thought we'd spend some time together.'

'We can!' said David. 'You could stay in the flat!'

David's flat was awful and barely big enough for one, and they both knew it. Maggie's housekeeping skills weren't up to much either.

'I should maybe go home,' said Maggie, finally, admitting defeat. 'Catch up with the folks.'

He nodded, pulling out a large pile of marking.

'Say hi to Stan for me,' he said, mournfully.

'That's not fair,' said Maggie. He looked at her, his dark eyes sad.

'Nothing's fair,' he said. 'That's why I'm staying behind.'

'You'll always put the kids ahead of me,' said Maggie.

'You sound like Miranda,' said David. And Maggie stormed out of the room.

Chapter Forty

The Prossers senior were frankly amazed. The weather over Easter was wonderful, and normally they would have expected Fliss to be stomping around the place, complaining about how bored she was and how rubbish everything was.

Instead, she was in the garden, under a large hat, studying, with a faintly dreamy expression on her face. When they'd asked her how Outward Bound had been, instead of scowling like they'd have expected, and muttering something about how they wouldn't understand, she had smiled, and said it was all right thanks. She'd shaped her terrible hair into something approaching a very short bob that looked gamine and cute on her, and, to everyone's amazement, even smiled from time to time. Hattie, neck-deep in A-level revision, gave her suspicious looks from time to time, but Fliss didn't even seem that interested in winding her up.

Simone, too, was busy as a bee as ever helping her dad in the restaurant and double studying her notes, just in case she'd missed anything, which she hadn't, and sending little catch-ups to Calvin all the time, and having Ash to stay (he had to stay in her brother's room, which he didn't mind, although Joel very much did).

Ash was fiercely jealous and suspicious of her friendship with Calvin, while being oddly impressed by it at the same time. Simone did not, she found, mind in the slightest Ash thinking she had lots of options. And the sheer gush of relief in finding she had fitted in on the Outward Bound, after three solid years of feeling she would never fit in anywhere, nurtured something inside her. She chatted to Happy and Patricia and Carey on WhatsApp, made plans for the summer term, and genuinely felt pleased with her lot – apart from terrible nightmares where she went to sit her GCSEs and found she was taking them in a language she didn't understand, and they were going to take her scholarship away, and her usual struggle to find nice jeans in a 16, given that she wasn't too sure what trendy jeans were supposed to look like anyway, and she had to wear a black skirt and a white shirt in the restaurant, which was practically a school uniform anyway so how was she supposed to know?

Apart from that, she was as happy a sixteen-year-old as her parents had ever seen her. They thought she had finally come round to the school's way of thinking; it would not have occurred to them, city dwellers through and through, that a bit of fresh air had helped more than all the books and teaching in the world.

Alice skied like a demon through the crisp slopes of Gstaad, joined the partying late into the night with a large group of her sister's friends, and ignored the tiny voice inside her that told her the exams were imminent. She was smart, she'd always managed to scrape by on brains alone before. Anyway, did she want to become a serious bluestocking like Miss Adair, always fretting about stupid things like exams that didn't matter at all? Of course not. There was fun to be had, grown-up fun, and she was going to have it. She smiled alluringly at the very hot, rough ski guide.

Ismé lay in her bed, angrily making notes on the curriculum. White male, white male, white male. It never ended. She would do well if she tried, of course she would. She could already feel herself being stretched, challenged at the school, seeing a whole raft of horizons opening up ahead of her. She knew that. And she knew the school was about solidity, about not changing.

But even so.

Chapter Forty-one

'I do not understand you,' said Claire in horror. For Easter she was catching the Eurostar to Paris after spending the night at the London Ritz with a new lover she refused to discuss even with Maggie.

'You are going to see your ex-lover?'

Maggie shrugged.

'You know, in France, David could kill you and not go to prison.'

Maggie looked so sad, packing her case that Friday.

Claire wrinkled her perfect tiny nose.

'*Pourquoi?* Stanley, he is dead to you. *Poubelle!*'

'I'm not going to see him! I'm going to see my family.'

She would go. Catch up with friends. Spend some time with her mother.

Then figure out what to do with the rest of her life.

If she and David hadn't broken up yet, it could only be because he hadn't had the nerve.

'So, ees over with man on horse?' said Claire, not unsympathetically.

'He just ... he's never there for me.'

'Perhaps he thinks you love thees other man.'

'He *can't*,' said Maggie fiercely. 'I gave up everything! My entire life for him! All my friends, my family, everything! And he gives me nothing, says nothing, wangs on about school all the time. Never about me. I have absolutely no idea where I stand, none. And I can't ... I can't waste my life on him any more, while he reads books and quotes poems and never ever speaks his mind. Honestly. I am ... I might be ... done.'

Claire tilted her head.

Maggie closed her eyes, kissed her friend goodbye, and headed to the station. It was rammed. Everyone joyfully getting away for the Easter break. Off to see friends and family and loved ones.

She sighed, and rolled her bag along. Behind her there was a commotion. Several people sniffed and gasped. Maggie turned around. A large, stupid-looking dog, off its leash, was bouncing around the station, highly excited at the combination of lots of interesting-smelling people and lots of food outlets.

'Oi!' a guard was shouting. 'Whose dog is that! Get him!', as the dog cavorted into WH Smiths.

Maggie smiled and turned away, checking her connection on the overhead board.

Then she looked back. It couldn't be.

Stephen Dedalus spotted her, and romped up to her, tail wagging furiously. There was a note tucked in his collar.

I am still banned from the station. But please ... please come outside.

'Take that bloody dog out and keep it under control!' the station manager was shouting at her. 'It could hurt a child!'

'I ... he couldn't ... ' said Maggie.

'Well, we only have your word for that.'

'I realise that, I'm—'

'He needs a lead.'

'I . . .'

Maggie realised it was pointless arguing, and took him outside, holding onto his collar, and letting him pull her wherever he wanted to go: presumably he knew where David was.

He was standing outside, on the old cobbled taxi rank, facing the station, looking utterly forlorn.

'Are you really still banned?' she said, glancing at her watch.

'Technically, not really,' he said. 'But I didn't want to risk it in case I made an idiot of myself again. They all know me.'

Maggie frowned.

'But what are you doing here? Are you liable to make an idiot of yourself?'

'Oh yes,' said David. And he held up his old, very battered copy of *Great Expectations*.

'What is that?' said Maggie, completely thrown.

'Whenever I try and talk to you,' said David, 'I can't. I can't get it out. I just can't do it. I'm sorry. I know that makes me a coward. But please. Just let me.'

'Wha—'

In answer, he just held the book up.

I loved her against reason, against promise, against peace, against hope, against happiness, against all discouragement that could be.

He turned to another page.

Love her, love her, love her! If she favours you, love her. If she wounds you, love her. If she tears your heart to pieces – and as it gets older and stronger, it will tear deeper – love her, love her, love her!

232

Maggie couldn't stop laughing, while crying at the same time.

'OK, OK, I get it! I get it! Oh my God, you are so mad having to use other people's words all the time. Just tell me!'

'I know. I know. I know. But do you get what I mean though?'

'Yes!'

'And . . . '

Painfully, anxiously, he put the book down. It was hard for him to say.

'I love you. I really do, Maggie.'

She gazed at him, everything forgiven.

'Do you love me?'

She looked at him, eyes brimming.

'Of course I do, you absolute plum.'

Chapter Forty-two

They jumped on the train in the end, all three of them, happiness spilling from them like stardust, dug up some fizz somehow from the buffet car, and they toasted each other, pouring out everything that had been in their hearts for the last few months, everything they had not managed to say, including, but not limited to, an emergency phone call from Claire shouting at him a mere hour before.

She rested her head on his shoulder, staring at the beautiful gentle fields of England, that would give way to the wild heights of the Lake District, and then the bright green rolling hills of home.

'I can take the weekend,' said David. 'At least I owe you that. I'm so so sorry.'

'Did you bring any marking?'

'Not a whit.'

She smiled and nestled into his sleeve.

'I thought . . . I thought you'd gone off me.'

'I know,' said David. 'Can we just put everything down to my being English?'

'What did Claire tell you?'

He shrugged.

'Not sure. Something about murder and getting away with it?'

And she turned to him, and kissed him wholeheartedly as they crossed the border.

Astonishingly, the fourth hotel they tried had a cancellation. Maggie called her parents, trying not to giggle as she told them she'd be a bit delayed.

The hotel had a roaring fire in the grate (Easter was not as sunny in the north as the south) and, astoundingly, a four-poster bed, and they went straight to bed, ordering room service, and revelling in their happiness.

'Could we possibly find a place together?' said David. 'Please? That flat is killing me. As are the bills at Reuben's.'

'I would love that,' said Maggie, closing her eyes, feeling the stress draining out of her at last.

And they lay in front of the fire and talked and talked and talked, and David told her everything, about how it had felt when his mum died, and how he had found school so difficult, and how it had made him so desperate to change things. And she told him the truth: that she had been happy with Stan, but was so much happier with him; and they built castles in the air and dreamed of a happy home for them-selves, then googled rental prices in Cornwall and turned it off again as the prices showed up.

SUMMER TERM

Chapter Forty-three

Maggie stood at the entrance to the exam hall. The single desks were laid out immaculately, as if with a ruler. Miss Starling had seen to it, of course.

They were looking at finding a place together, the two of them. Maggie had her heart set on Looe, with its beaches and stunning views out over Mount Polbearne, the staggering half-submerged island that shimmered above the waves and let you walk there at low tide. They had lots to discuss. They'd need a little garden for Stephen Dedalus, which was expensive, but even so. She couldn't believe it; was regularly having to pinch herself. She was brimming, overflowing with happiness, revelling in the glories of the early summer. She had to remind herself to feel sorry for the girls, drawn and pale with studying, terrified of ploughing their exams; for Maggie, there were late nights, and interrupted sleep as she marked and re-marked, as the girls practised and practised old papers all over again. Bright pink and green spring was redolent of exam time; it had taken years for Maggie to shake off her fear of it.

And now, here they were; there was no more time, no room for extra prep. Everything they knew stored, teetering, in their heads, ready, hopefully, to flow all over the exam papers over the next three hours.

Simone Pribetich looked absolutely terrified, which was ridiculous – she had everything memorised. The only way she could do badly now was if one of the light fittings fell from the roof and rendered her unconscious. Although, to be fair to Simone, she was half worried about the exams and half worried about Ash, who had gone on at her relentlessly throughout the holiday about Calvin this and Calvin that, and was driving them both demented.

Felicity Prosser looked scared but defiant; her work had picked up, and she should do well. Alice flounced in like she hadn't a care in the world. Her creative essays, thought Maggie, who enjoyed them hugely – they read like a cross between Jackie Collins and Carrie Bradshaw – would probably carry her through.

'Good luck,' she said to them all individually as they filed in. 'You'll be great. You'll be fine.'

Ismé came in last, looking belligerent.

'Ismé,' said Maggie, taking her aside, 'I have this for you. I should have given it to you before, I'm sorry. I'm so glad you're here. I so hope ... I hope ...'

And she handed Ismé a piece of paper.

Over at Phillip Dean, David smiled desperately at his boys and girls, who sounded a lot more bullish. Some simply hadn't shown up at all, and for all his fussing, there was not very much he could do about that.

The rest were clowning around, hysterically laughing, moaning about forgotten pencil cases and all the rest of it. He studied them carefully. Kelisa was wearing trousers that looked sprayed on, but her expression was focused.

'You got this,' he said to her.

'Neh,' she said, screwing up her face.

'You do,' he said. 'You absolutely do.'

Calvin walked by.

'Take those headphones out!' ordered David.

Calvin grinned. 'Just revising my quotes,' he said. 'Simone sent me an audio file.'

'Did she?' said David. 'I'll be out of a job.'

He grinned.

'Remember. You have plenty of time. You know what to do. Go do it. For your nan.'

Calvin's face was thoughtful.

'If I do this . . . everything changes.'

'Yes, it does,' said David. 'But if you don't, it changes anyway. And I promise. My change is better.'

Calvin nodded soberly and entered. Young Silver came up.

'Go for it,' said David. Silver shrugged. 'I've got an apprenticeship,' he said, shyly.

David's face cracked into a beam. 'Silver! That's brilliant! Congratulations! Where?'

'Toyota.'

'No way! That is *brilliant*! I am so proud of you!'

'I can sort you out, sir. Get rid of that rust bucket you drive.'

'I like my Saab!'

'Yeah yeah,' said Silver, skipping in.

David watched them all in with a smile, handed over to the external invigilators with a nod, then retreated round the corner to call Maggie who, like him, was at least as nervous as the kids were. After that, he walked up and down.

Maggie knew she shouldn't be peering in the window of the exam hall, but she couldn't help herself. Ismé was writing furiously, almost certainly the same beautifully argued essay about decolonising the curriculum she had turned in for her mocks, that had scored her an A star then and would once more, even though she was theoretically answering a discursive essay question about government spending. Fliss was writing a strongly imagined romantic story about a boy from a rough school and a fragile girl from a smart school, in a pleasingly earnest style. Alice was staring out of the window, strumming her fingers. Simone was oblivious in a world of her own, writing so much that eventually the invigilators would pick the A out of the sea of available options.

A silence settled over every school in the land; a dusty stillness, punctuated by scribbling pens, the occasion creaking desk; the lifting of a hand, the quiet pace of soft-soled invigilators' feet, the toing and froing between the lines of desks; the occasional sighs of disappointment as the wrong question came up; muttered impatience; frustrated rubbings out; the slow, resolute tick of the big industrial clocks overhead, measuring out dreams and futures, second by second, moment by moment.

Chapter Forty-four

The last assembly of the year at Downeys was joint, with the boys and girls in together – and the Phillip Dean classes.

Dr Fisley's Downey-Dean choir performed 'Chasing Cars' to the entire school, including a smattering of Phillip Dean parents David had notified, and a few people felt a little tearful at the beautiful sound they made. Dr Deveral made a speech about how proud she was of everything they'd achieved, and how hard they had worked, in a difficult year.

Just as people were clapping, full of relief and looking ahead to the wonderful free summer ahead, there was a sudden commotion by the side of the stage.

A tiny boy who didn't look large enough to be a fourth year burst onto the platform.

It was Ash Mehta, brimming with pink righteous fury.

'I just wanted to announce,' he said into the microphone, 'that I turned sixteen yesterday. Therefore I now wish to . . . '

And to a growing sense of looming horror and laughter, he went down on one knee.

'Simone Pribetich. Will you marry me?'

Everyone stared at Simone.

'Go, girl!' yelled Calvin from the back of the hall. Alice burst out laughing. Maggie started forwards. Kelisa, Happy, Carey and Patricia all sighed with how romantic it was.

Simone half wanted the ground to swallow her up and to disappear completely.

And half ... was secretly rather pleased.

'Oh *God*!' said Fliss, horrified but delighted at the same time. 'OH MY GOD!'

Dr Deveral was moving forwards.

'I am not sure this is at all the appropriate place and time.'

'It is if you love someone!' said Ash, stoutly.

'He's got a point,' came a voice behind Maggie.

She whirled round.

David was standing there. She looked at him.

'What?'

'I'm just saying ...'

He looked at her very intently. Dr Fitzroy was now bundling Ash off the stage, to a chorus of boos, completely unsure as to whether Ash had in fact done something against school rules or not.

Maggie stared at David, who appeared to be ... he wasn't bending down. He couldn't be. He better not be.

'Don't! You! Dare!' she hissed. 'What the *hell* are you doing now?'

And then her phone rang. As Dr Fitzroy was dealing with Ash, she muted it. It rang again, immediately. David stared at her. 'Should you get that?'

Maggie stepped outside.

'Oh my God,' said Maggie. She lifted up her head. 'Oh my God. I wonder ... she knew I was coming here, that I'd be out of the way. Maybe that's why ... Maybe that's ...'

Tears pricked at the corners of her eyes.

'What's the matter?'

'Nothing,' she said firmly, furious with herself that she

couldn't control it, couldn't rein it back. 'Nothing at all. I just . . . I just wish that they'd told me first.'

'What *is* it?'

'Stan and Anne,' said Maggie, shaking her head. 'God. Of course. Why didn't I . . . God. I'm so stupid. I mean . . . I'm so . . . I'm so dumb. What was I even thinking?'

'What? Your sister Anne?'

Maggie nodded numbly.

'They're . . . they're engaged. They're getting married.'

Results

Ismé Elgar-Phipps	9 9 9 9 9 9 9 9 9 9
Simone Pribetich	9 9 9 9 9 9 9 9 9
Fliss Prosser	9 8 8 7 8 7 8 8 7
Alice Trebizon-Woods	6 5 6 6 7 6 6 6

Percentage of Downey House girls 9–4 grades   **97.2%**

| Calvin Hopekirk | 6 6 6 6 6 6 |
| Kelisa Davidson | 6 5 6 6 8 5 6 |

Percentage of Phillip Dean pupils 9–4 grades   **16.4%**
in English   **58.9%**

Paper handed by Maggie to Ismé
REVISED DOWNEY GIRLS GCSE CURRICULUM

The Color Purple	Alice Walker
The Empress	Tanika Gupta
Great Expectations	Charles Dickens
Coram Boy	Jamila Gavin
Boys Don't Cry	Malorie Blackman
Othello	William Shakespeare
No Problem	Benjamin Zephaniah
The Emigrée	Carol Rumens
Tissue	Imtiaz Dharker
Dusting the Phone	Jackie Kay

Downey House Boys' School
Adleford,
Cornwall EX75

Blessing Hopekirk
Flat 27a
Eddings Tower
Exeter EX12

31 August 2022

Dear Ms Hopekirk,

I am delighted to inform you, as the guardian of Calvin Hopekirk, that he has been awarded a full scholarship to Downey Boys' School, commencing September this year. The scholarship includes transport, full boarding and a clothing allowance. His sporting excellence we hope will show itself on the field hockey team following his successful try-outs, and we believe he will become a valued and respected member of our school.

Please find enclosed some forms which should be returned in the next week or so. If you have any questions, please telephone my secretary on the number given,

We are so looking forward to welcoming Calvin at the start of term,

Yours sincerely,

Dr Robert Fitzroy
Headmaster

Acknowledgements

Thanks: Jo Unwin; Lucy Malagoni, Darcy Nicholson, Milly Reilly, Joanna Kramer, Zoe Carroll, Charlie King, David Shelley, Stephanie Melrose, Gemma Shelley, and all at Little, Brown; Deborah Schneider and Rachel Kahan at William Morrow; Wendy McLay.

Particular thanks to regular readers of this series. Whenever I give a talk if there are fifty people there, on average two will be 'Class' readers, and you mean a lot to me.

Escape with
JENNY COLGAN

In a quaint seaside resort, where the air is rich with
the smell of fresh buns and bread, a charming bakery
holds the key to another world…

'Deliciously warm and sweet'
SOPHIE KINSELLA

Escape with
JENNY COLGAN

Escape to a remote little Scottish island and meet the charmingly eccentric residents of Mure...

'Charming, made me long to escape to Mure. Total joy'
SOPHIE KINSELLA

Escape with
JENNY COLGAN

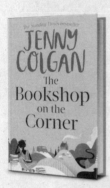
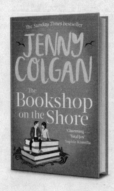

Nestled amidst the gorgeous Scottish Highlands lies
a magical world of books and romance...

'Gorgeous location, dancing dialogue and
characters you'll fall in love with. Irresistible!'
JILL MANSELL

Escape with
JENNY COLGAN

Meet Issy Randall, proud owner of the most enchanting café the world has ever seen, who is about to discover that running her own business isn't as easy as she thought…

'Sheer indulgence from start to finish'
SOPHIE KINSELLA

Escape with
JENNY COLGAN

In a delightful little sweet shop, pocket money jangles,
paper bags rustle and, behind the many rows of jars,
secret dreams lie in wait…

'An evocative sweet treat'
JOJO MOYES

~ DREAM WITH ~

JENNY COLGAN

Keep in touch with Jenny and her readers:

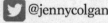 JennyColganBooks   @jennycolgan

JennyColganBooks

Check out Jenny's website and sign up to her newsletter for
all the latest book news plus mouth-watering recipes.

www.jennycolgan.com

LOVE TO READ?

Join **The Little Book Café** for competitions,
sneak peeks and more.

 TheLittleBookCafe   @littlebookcafe